Lucy Tryon

Whiz Reilly

Babs Reilly

Marie Macpherson,
25, Ross Avenue
Inverness

GINNY GORDON

and the

Mystery at the Old Barn

By
JULIE CAMPBELL

Illustrated by
MARGARET JERVIS

WHITMAN PUBLISHING COMPANY
RACINE, WISCONSIN

CONTENTS

CHAPTER		PAGE
I.	A Mysterious Envelope	9
II.	The Ballad Singer	25
III.	Babs in Trouble	37
IV.	A Threat	55
V.	A Hidden Weapon	67
VI.	A Broken Window	80
VII.	More Bad News	90
VIII.	The Missing Sandwiches	103
IX.	"We've Been Robbed!"	114
X.	Bread and Glue	127
XI.	The Inn's Ghost	142
XII.	Night Visitors	155
XIII.	The Long, White Envelope	166
XIV.	Clues and a Composition	179
XV.	Cause for Worry	194
XVI.	Wire, Film, and a Flash Bulb	205
XVII.	An Unwelcome Caller	218
XVIII.	The End and a Beginning	232

"I'm Getting Stage Fright," Ginny Said

GINNY GORDON
and the
Mystery at the Old Barn

CHAPTER ONE

A MYSTERIOUS ENVELOPE

"I'm getting stage fright," Ginny said to her best friend, Lucy Tryon. "If someone doesn't come soon I'll scream."

"Why, Ginny Gordon," Lucy gasped, her blue eyes wide with surprise. "I didn't know you had a nerve in your body."

For the tenth time in the last half-hour, Ginny inspected her pretty face in the mirror behind the sandwich counter. She patted her chestnut curls and her big brown eyes frowned back at her.

"Oh, I know," she told her reflection. "Now I've got to wash my hands again. That's the trouble with being in the restaurant business. There are so many laws I never knew existed."

"If you wash your hands one more time," John Blaketon said from the soft-drink counter on the opposite side of the Barn, "you won't have any skin left." He smiled.

Ginny nervously pinched the ruffles of the gay

red-and-white checked apron which she was wearing over her blue wool frock.

"What time is it, John?" she asked. "Suppose nobody shows up?"

"It's just four," John told her, glancing at his wrist watch. "The place will be packed and jammed soon. After the swell write-up your father gave us, we can't miss."

Ginny's father owned the Harristown *News*. For the past three weeks, Ginny and the other Hustlers, as they called themselves, had worked hard after school and week-ends renovating an abandoned barn on the estate of John's grandmother, old Mrs. Blaketon.

John, who was fifteen, a year older than Ginny, was the president of the club, and Ginny was treasurer. He was in charge of soft drinks, and his thirteen-year-old cousins, the redheaded Reilly twins, were to wait on the tables.

On the shelves behind the counter which John had made, were stacks of sandwiches neatly wrapped in wax paper. Ginny and Lucy had spent the whole beautiful, sunny, October Saturday afternoon making them. In the refrigerator were several pounds of sliced cheese and hamburger patties. The big room from the floor to the rafters was spick-and-span.

The Snack Barn was ready for business, and Ginny was suddenly sure that not one single customer would show up.

"I don't think we should have spent so much money on perishables," she said in a discouraged tone of voice. "The cheese slices will dry out into cardboard strips if nobody shows up, and the hamburger won't keep long even in our electric refrigerator."

"We've got to specialize in cheeseburgers," plump Babs Reilly said. "The Junior-Senior High crowd never buys anything else at the Grill or the Inn."

"They can't afford to buy anything else at the Inn," Whiz told her. "But unless we want to be sued for plagiarism, we'd better not fix 'em exactly the way the Grill does."

"But they're so divine with pickles and coleslaw," Lucy wailed. Lucy was almost as plump as the always-hungry twins. "Besides, I don't think swiping recipes comes under the heading of plagiarism, does it, John?"

John shook his head, smiling. "Of course not. Besides, we're not going to serve our cheeseburgers exactly the way the Inn and the Grill serve theirs, are we, Ginny?"

"Not unless we run out of Riba's divine homemade relish," Ginny said, mentally counting the number of jars in the wall cupboard behind her. "Honestly, John," she complained, "I know Riba has been your grandmother's maid ever since they were both young girls, and you all feel she's one of the Blaketon family, but—"

"But," John finished with a grin, "she was un-co-operative about giving us credit when it came to her relishes, jams, and jellies?"

"Un-co-operative," Ginny said, "is putting it mildly. She was downright suspicious, even when I showed her the cute little 'Riba' stickers Dad had made for us." Ginny pointed to the gay red, white, and blue label on a large jar of relish beside a platter of sliced cheese. "I thought she'd be flattered when she saw that we'd put her name on all of them except the few we had made especially for your salad dressing, John."

John was not only an excellent amateur cabinet-maker; he had concocted a delicious salad dressing which the Hustlers hoped to sell as a side line along with Riba's products.

"Riba," Whiz said with a chuckle, "probably got the word label mixed up with the word libel. She's naturally suspicious anyway. I remember when Babs and I were kids we were parked on Granny one summer while Mother and Dad took a vacation away from us."

"A well-needed vacation, I might add," John said.

Whiz ignored his cousin who was two years older. "Riba," he went on as though he hadn't been interrupted, "wouldn't go into my room to clean it because I had an electric clock."

"Whiz," Babs put in, "was a wizard at electricity even then. He made the clock himself."

"I only repaired it," Whiz corrected her. "And it made a ghastly whirring noise. Riba was convinced that it was a time bomb."

"It probably was, in a way," John said with a grin. "In those days you were always blowing fuses with your crazy inventions."

"Practice makes perfect," freckle-faced Whiz said airily. "If I hadn't experimented in my youth, we wouldn't be serving cheeseburgers this afternoon. Who rebuilt that secondhand refrigerator, may I ask, and who made that battered old electric stove work?"

"You're really wonderful," Ginny said. "But don't forget that John built the counters and shelves and cupboards, and made all our darling rustic tables and benches out of odd pieces of pine he picked up cheap at the lumber yard."

"I painted them," Babs said. "At least I helped."

"Stained is the word," John told her. "If they'd been painted they wouldn't look rustic."

"Stained is right," Lucy added ruefully. "In the end we paid more money for turpentine than we did for the stain, and my hands—"

"Money," Ginny interrupted, "is what worries me. As treasurer and business manager of the Harristown Snack Barn, I have to confess that I've got the jitters. We haven't nearly as much capital left in our savings account as the rest of you seem to think."

"Wha-at?" Whiz clutched his unruly red hair. "If I seem to think correctly, we should have about three hundred dollars."

"That," Ginny informed him tartly, "is because you don't even *seem* to think correctly. You've got to admit that you're only interested in the electrical end of any project we go into, Whiz." She smiled at him. "We started out with the five hundred dollars Mrs. Arnold paid us for the good will of the Swap Shop when we turned it over to Joe Dakor. And Joe, even though he's a licensed electrician, charged us practically nothing for wiring this barn and install- ing lights and the automatic hot water heater."

Whiz nodded. "I paid almost nothing for the Victrola, stove, and refrigerator."

"That's right," Ginny said, "but the electrical end of opening this restaurant wasn't everything. The old plumbing had to be repaired and the sinks put in."

"How much?" Whiz asked anxiously.

"About a hundred dollars," Ginny told him. Whiz whistled.

"And," John added, "even odds and ends of wood run into money, not to mention nails, plastic wood, glue and such."

"That old-fashioned ice box for your soft drinks," Babs told John, "didn't cost a cent. Granny said we could have it when she gave us those boxes of china and kitchenware I found in her attic."

"But don't forget glasses and knives and forks and spoons," Lucy pointed out. "I spent twenty dollars in Shoemaker's basement and the ten-cent store for things like that. You know, paper napkins, dish towels, straws, and spatulas. I ran out of money before I got through the list. That's why I bought only one ten-cent can opener although we really should have two."

"I'm really frightened," Ginny admitted. "I spent over twenty dollars for supplies at the grocery store today. Of course, the canned goods and soft drinks will keep indefinitely if we don't open them, but I wish we hadn't bought quite so many perishables. Suppose nobody shows up today? We'll have to pour most of the ice cream down the sink. The freezing compartment of our refrigerator isn't as large as it should be."

"We won't pour any of it down the sink," Babs said firmly. "I'll eat every drop of it if it kills me."

"Which it would," Whiz said, trying to grin in spite of his worry. "How much capital *have* we left, Ginny?"

Ginny sighed. "Fifty-five dollars and ninety-three cents. I didn't want to break the bad news until after the opening today," she said. "But since it's after four now and the announcement in the *News* said we'd be open for business at four—" Suddenly she couldn't stand it any longer. She ducked under the counter and hurried to the door to stare down the shady lane which ran between the woods and the fields, sloping up from the main road.

And then she saw them. It looked as though every boy and girl who went to the Harristown Junior-Senior High was bicycling up the lane.

"Here they come," Ginny yelled as she dashed back to her place behind the sandwich counter. "Whiz! Babs! Don't you dare eat a morsel of the food you bring to the tables. Oh, Lucy, it looks as though we didn't make nearly enough sandwiches after all. And, John, I'm sure you didn't order a big enough chunk of ice."

They all laughed at Ginny's abrupt change of attitude, and from then on they were too busy to worry about the money end of their business. It seemed to the Hustlers as though everyone who lived in or near the little New York suburb stopped in for at least a sandwich and a cup of tea that warm October afternoon. Even old Mrs. Arnold came, leaning on the arm of her chauffeur, Carson, who was a good friend of the Hustlers.

"I declare, Ginny," the little old lady said enthusiastically as she finished her third cheeseburger. "You get smarter every day. That Swap Shop of yours was a stroke of genius, and this Snack Barn is just what our teen-agers need." She shook her head sadly. "In my day fourteen-year-old girls didn't have your gumption."

"I'm sure *you* had plenty," Ginny said, smiling.

"I'm glad you approve of the Barn. We hope like anything that it'll be a success because, you know, we don't plan to keep it for ourselves; we want it to become a community project."

"It's a big success right now," Mrs. Arnold said, glancing around at the crowded tables and wall benches. "I can't get over what you've done to Nelly Blaketon's old barn. It's got great charm. I love the little red-and-white checked curtains which match the aprons you and Lucy and Babs are wearing."

"Lucy made them," Ginny said. "She's the seamstress of our club. She covered the cushions, too. I can't even baste evenly."

"I can't either," Mrs. Arnold admitted with a chuckle. "What are you going to do after the town takes over your Barn, Ginny?"

"Do you think it really will work out that way?" Ginny asked.

"Of course, it will," Mrs. Arnold assured her. "Girls and boys your age need a clubhouse of their own where they can get between-meal snacks. This is the ideal place." She added in a whisper, "I've got a scheme. When the town takes over here, come to me. I've always wanted to have a finger in one of your pies, Ginny. Next time you've got to let me."

"I will," Ginny promised.

Just then old Mrs. Blaketon hobbled in with her withered little maid, Riba. Shortly after that Ginny's Great-Aunt Betsy appeared, escorted by her two old servants, Rachel and Franklin. Ginny was so surprised to see her great-aunt who seldom left her home, that she could hardly speak. But Whiz, with a flourish of the snowy white napkin he carried over one arm, seated all three of the old ladies at one table where they were soon hobnobbing about old times.

Carson's pretty young fiancée, Betty Leland, came in with Officer Bill. The big, burly policeman stopped at both counters to deliver brief lectures to Ginny and John. "Don't you forget a word the Public Health Inspector told you," he warned Ginny. "I'm coming out regularly to check up on you."

"Please do," Ginny said with a laugh as she added the fifty-cent piece he gave her to the mounting pile of change in the cash box. "If you test everything we serve in the Barn every day, we'll soon be rich."

"You'll never be rich, Ginny Gordon," the friendly policeman said, grinning. "You spend too much time getting mixed up in mysteries which don't concern you."

Lucy handed Officer Bill the cheeseburger she had just made for him. "That's not true," she said. "Every mystery Ginny has been mixed up in so far has concerned us all. That ex-convict, Tolliver Graham, was trying to make us give up the Swap Shop. And if Ginny hadn't found out who stole Mrs. Arnold's missing heirloom, we would have been blamed for losing it."

"True, true," Officer Bill said genially. "Well, nobody's going to run you out of here except a Health Department officer. And he won't, unless I report that you're creating a nuisance." Munching his sandwich, he glanced thoughtfully around the crowded room, and then left.

"Oh, dear," Ginny whispered to Lucy. "He really did inspect the Barn carefully today. I hope we didn't break any rules."

"There are so many of them," Lucy moaned. "John told me that the screened door cost fifteen dollars even though he made it himself. If it wasn't so unseasonably hot, we could have got by with just the solid wood door."

"I know," Ginny agreed. "It's a nuisance having to make sure that the screened door is closed all the time we're serving food instead of just hooking it back. But as soon as it gets really cold we won't have to worry about flies."

At six o'clock the crowd began to dwindle, and by seven everyone had gone except the Hustlers.

"I'm so hungry," Babs wailed, "I could eat the crust Doctor Bascom's teething baby played with!"

"That's about all there is left to eat," Whiz said, stacking the last plates in the sink. "But thank goodness a square meal awaits us at home. Let's go, twin."

"Well, the nerve of them," Lucy said as she watched them bike down the lane. "They were supposed to dry the dishes and put them away."

"Well," Ginny said wearily, "they *were* good about not eating a thing. We might as well let them off this once."

John was rinsing glasses at the other sink. "If they hadn't been kept so busy serving, they would have eaten up all our profits," he said. "How much do you think we made, Ginny?"

"I haven't the vaguest idea," Ginny replied. "But the cash box is overflowing, and we only had about ten dollars in change to start with."

After they had finished tidying the Barn, Ginny pulled a stool to the section of the counter where they kept the cash box. "Counting all this will take time," she said. "You two go along home. I'm so sick of the sight of food I couldn't eat dinner. And I'm dying to know how much money we took in."

"I'll help you, Ginny," John offered. He glanced at his wrist watch. "I'm sorry, I'll have to take that back. We're having dinner at the Inn tonight and they start serving at eight. We might lose our table if I'm late, so I'd better scram." He shrugged into his jacket. "It's dark out now, Ginny. I don't like the idea of your biking down the lane alone later. Will you stay with her, Lucy?"

"I can't," Lucy said. "I promised Mother I'd be home at eight. She's having dinner late tonight especially on account of our opening, so I've got to be on time."

"We're having dinner late for the same reason," Ginny said, "but I told Mother not to wait for me. I'll have some cookies and a glass of milk before I go to bed. She said it was all right as long as I'm home by nine."

John hooked back the screened door, and Lucy hurried out. "I'll eat and run, Ginny," he said. "Wait here for me. I'll be back in about forty-five minutes. Will you be through with your bookkeeping by then?"

Ginny nodded, too busy counting the money to look up. When she finished counting it, she discovered that they had taken in more than thirty-three dollars. Then she took an inventory of what was left in stock and decided that they had made a profit of about sixteen dollars.

"A swell beginning," she said to herself as she began to close and lock the windows. "If only we can keep on like this!"

"Good evening," a voice interrupted from the darkness of the doorway.

Ginny jumped. A tall, well-dressed man moved suavely into the room. He glanced around and said in a disappointed tone of voice, "It looks as though you'd closed up."

"Oh, we have," Ginny told him, wondering who he could be. "Didn't you read the notice in the *News?* We stop serving food at five-thirty and close the door at seven. Sundays we're only open from ten to three—for brunch, you know." She smiled at him tiredly. "I'm only here this late because I'm the treasurer."

He smiled back at her. "Then you must be Miss Ginny Gordon. My name is Chadwell."

"I'm awfully sorry, Mr. Chadwell," Ginny said. "Did you come all the way out here expecting dinner?"

"Not exactly," he said. "I merely made an arrangement with a friend of mine. I'm to leave something here with you which he'll pick up later." He drew a long, thick white envelope from the inside pocket of his topcoat. "Henderson is his name and he's very anxious to receive this. May I leave it with you?"

"Well," Ginny said doubtfully. "I won't be here much longer myself."

"He'll be here any minute now," Mr. Chadwell assured her. "As I just said, he's very, very anxious to get the contents of this envelope."

"All right," Ginny said, taking the envelope he held out to her. "Should Mr. Henderson give me some identification before I turn it over to him?"

"He certainly should," Mr. Chadwell said with a cold smile. "In fact, you are not to turn it over to him unless he *first* gives you five one-thousand-dollar bills."

"Five thousand dollars!" Ginny gasped. "Oh, Mr. Chadwell, I couldn't possibly be responsible for any-

"May I Leave This Envelope With You?"

thing as valuable as that. Suppose Mr. Henderson doesn't arrive before I leave?"

"But he will," Mr. Chadwell said confidently. He started for the door. "I'll drive out from New York tomorrow morning as early as I can to pick up the money."

"Wait a minute, please," Ginny called after him. "What am I supposed to do with all that money until you come back for it?"

But he had already disappeared into the darkness. For several minutes Ginny was too stunned to move. Then she ducked under the counter and hurried to the door. It was pitch dark outside and silent except for the rustling of the trees in the woods.

"Oh, dear," Ginny groaned. "He's gone and I'm stuck with this envelope." She went back to the counter and put it in the cash box. "Why do I always get myself into these involved situations?" she asked herself. "John will have a fit when he hears about it. I wonder what can be keeping him anyway. It must be nearly nine and it isn't like John to be late, especially when he told me to wait for him."

Ginny finished locking the windows and then she heard someone walking up the lane from the main road. Suddenly she felt weak and shaky all over. Suppose it wasn't John? Suppose it was Mr. Henderson? What on earth would she do with the five thousand dollars he was going to give her?

CHAPTER TWO

THE BALLAD SINGER

Ginny stared down at her shaking hands. "Stop it," she scolded herself. "There's absolutely nothing to be nervous about. If whoever is coming up the lane turns out to be Mr. Henderson, he'll give you the money and you'll give him the envelope. Then when John arrives you can dump the whole thing on his responsible shoulders."

"Ginny!" It was John's voice!

Ginny's nervousness fled as rapidly as it had come. "For goodness sake, John," she said crossly as he came in the door. "What kept you? Mother and Dad are going to give me an awful bawling out when I get home. I would have left without waiting for you, but the cash box is so heavy and I didn't dare leave all that money here."

"I'm sorry, Ginny," John said contritely. "But you won't get bawled out by your family. I called them up and explained."

"Explained what?" Ginny demanded. "It had better be good. Mother is none too happy about the Snack Barn anyway. She keeps reminding me of the two narrow escapes I had while we were running the Swap Shop."

"I can't say that I blame her." John's blue eyes were dark with seriousness. "Remember your promise. If you get involved in another mystery, don't leave me out of it until it's almost too late."

Ginny tossed her chestnut curls. "Oh, for heaven's sake, John, you sound as though you were fifty instead of fifteen." She pushed the cash box toward him. "We took in about thirty-three dollars, mostly silver. What are we going to do with it between now and lunch time Monday which is the first chance I'll get to put it in the bank?"

"Thirty-three dollars?" John whistled. "Boy, that's swell, Ginny. I wish I thought we could take in that much every Saturday."

"There's no reason why we shouldn't," Ginny told him. "Of course, a lot of the older people only came today to be nice. I still don't see how Mrs. Arnold, your granny, and my Great-Aunt Betsy tottered all the way up the lane from the main road. And I'll bet they never try it again." She chuckled. "But next Saturday we'll start serving lunches, so I don't see any reason—"

"There is a reason, Ginny," John said soberly. "And it's also the reason why I was late. I'll tell you about it on the way home."

Ginny sighed. "I can guess. Babs has got into one of her usual scrapes which means she and Whiz won't be allowed to wait on the tables any more, which means we'll have to hire waitresses, which means we'll be broke before we even get started."

John laughed. "No, at the moment the twins are not in the doghouse." He opened the cash box and stared at the envelope Ginny had laid on top of the neatly arranged money. "What's that?"

"Never mind," Ginny said wearily. "I'm too exhausted to explain now. Just answer me one question before I fall asleep on my feet. Are we going to take all that money home, or leave it here?"

John ran his fingers through his black, wavy hair. "It's probably perfectly safe here," he said after a minute. "But I suppose we really shouldn't leave more than five dollars in change locked in the cash box overnight, should we?"

"*I* don't think so," Ginny said. "Officer Bill told me once that tramps traveling along the main highway often sleep in the woods across the lane. On rainy nights they may have slept in here before you fixed the door. And if one of them wanted to do it now all he would have to do is break in through a window. Once he's inside—" She shrugged, too tired to finish the sentence.

"Tramps don't break into locked barns, not as a rule," John said thoughtfully. "But to be on the safe side, let's never leave more than a few dollars in change here overnight. I'll be responsible for the rest of it over the week-end, if you like."

"I like it very much," Ginny said tiredly. "You have a wallet, and I haven't." She took a pad of petty cash vouchers from the box and handed it to John. "Write down whatever you take and sign the slip. It's not that I don't trust you, Mr. Blaketon, but we've got to run this Snack Barn in a businesslike way if we're going to get anywhere."

John stared at her. "I've never seen you in such a sour mood before, Ginny, and I've known you all of your life. What's the matter? Something worrying you?"

Ginny nodded. She *was* tired. It had been a long exciting day, and deep down inside her she knew that if she hadn't been so tired she would never have let Mr. Chadwell leave that envelope in her care. She wanted more than anything else in the world just then to tell John all about it and let him shoulder the responsibility. But, before he shouldered it, he would express his disapproval. Ginny was quite sure that she faced a scolding when she got home. A scolding from John first would be the straw that broke the camel's back. At the moment she felt as though she would burst into tears if anyone said a cross word to her.

So, instead of going into details she simply said, "I am worried, John. And it has something to do with that envelope. But please don't ask me why now."

John smiled sympathetically. "You've worked hard all day, Ginny, and you've had the extra responsibility of handling the money. Let's go," he said, leading the way outside. He handed her the flashlight he had brought with him. "Just hold this while I snap the bow of the padlock. Then we can forget about the Barn until tomorrow."

But, as they trundled their bikes down the dark lane he added, "I'm worried, too, Ginny. I'm afraid we won't be in business very long."

"But why?" Ginny demanded. "We've started out so well, and everyone raved about the food, and they all said how attractive the place was. When you finish building the Ping-pong table—"

"I'm not going to work on it any more," John said in a discouraged tone of voice. "It would just be a waste of time now."

Ginny laid her hand lightly on his arm. "You're tired too, John. It's not like you to give up so easily."

"I'm not giving up," John said. "But there really isn't any sense in our competing with the Inn."

"The Inn?" Ginny gasped in amazement. "What ever gave you the idea that we're competing with the Inn? Why, it's so famous for its cooking, people from New York pack and jam it every week-end." They had reached the brightly lighted highway now and Ginny stared up at him. "I think you've lost your mind, John. One of the reasons we thought of having a snack bar for the high-school crowd is that there just isn't any place to eat in Harristown except the Inn and the All Night Grill. The Grill isn't attractive and the Inn is too expensive. Why, they charge fifty cents for a measly little sandwich and a small Coke, just for the privilege of eating in such a famous place."

"The Inn," John said soberly, "is going to be famous for something else besides its food pretty soon."

"For what?" Ginny asked impatiently as they biked toward the park. "It's just a great big old rambling frame mansion that once belonged to a governor or somebody important a hundred years ago. I suppose you could say the high ceilings give it atmosphere, but our crowd doesn't go for that sort of atmosphere. They like cozy places like the Barn, with a Victrola where they can play their favorite hillbilly records. Why, the Inn hasn't even a juke box."

"It's got something better than that now," John told her. "I hate to depress you, Ginny," he went on, "but this afternoon the Inn hired a ballad singer straight from the 'Kaintuck mountings.' Boy, is he a wow! Accompanies himself on the accordion, and had everybody swooning all over the place when he performed during dinner this evening."

Ginny was so surprised she braked her bike to a stop and got off it. "A hillbilly singer with an accordion! Oh, *no,* John. We *are* ruined."

John jumped off his own bike. "I'm afraid so, Ginny. That's why I was late coming back for you this evening. When this Lochinvar appeared with the shrimp cocktail, I all but swooned myself. He's got just about everything. Tall, dark, and handsome, is putting it mildly. And when he sings and plays—well, you never heard anything like it. Even Mother and Dad, who, as you know, go in for the opera and such, thought he was out of this world. I'm telling you, Ginny," he finished, "once the highschool crowd catches on that for a mere fifty cents—"

"Don't say anything more, puh-leeze," Ginny moaned. "I suppose this Kentucky Lochinvar is going to perform during the hours we planned to lure the gang to the Barn?"

John nodded. "While Dad was paying the check I went back and spoke to the manager. Mr. Crayne was very nice, and all that. Said he knew we had just opened the Snack Barn and that he had no intention of cutting in on our business, but this Lochinvar had made him a simply fabulous offer which he couldn't turn down."

They trundled their bikes along the short cut through the park toward Maple Street where Ginny lived. "How do you mean, fabulous?" she asked John.

"According to Mr. Crayne," John told her, "Lochinvar offered to entertain during lunch, teatime and dinner five days a week in exchange for room and board. All he wants is a small salary for entertaining during the same hours over the week-ends." He shrugged hopelessly. "There go our after-school snacks, our Saturday lunches and Sunday brunches."

"Lochinvar," Ginny repeated and quoted from Scott's *Marmion*,

" 'For lady's suit and minstrel's strain,
    By knight should ne'er be heard in vain.'
Is that his real name, John?"

"I have no idea," John said. "But if he called himself Dracula it wouldn't make any diff. He's that good."

"For pity's sake," Ginny groaned. "If Lochinvar is as good as you say he is, why doesn't he go and get himself a job in New York?"

"That I can't answer," John admitted. "Frankly, I think he would make a fortune in the movies, and if he wanted to become a prize fighter he'd be the world's champion in no time. You never saw such a perfect physical specimen, Ginny."

"That does it," she said mournfully. "He'll be the dream man of all the high-school girls and the hero of all the boys before we know it."

"Not to mention the fact," John added, "that he sings like a lark and accompanies himself on the accordion."

"I hope he chokes on a fish bone," Ginny said bitterly. Then she squared her shoulders resolutely. "Let's not cross any bridges till we come to them, John. Who knows, some Hollywood scout may snap your Lochinvar up before the teen-age gang catches on."

"That's our only hope," John admitted. "Mr.

Crayne told me that Lochinvar refused to sign a contract."

"You certainly had a heart-to-heart talk with the Inn's manager," Ginny said. "I suppose that's why you were so late coming back to the Barn for me."

John nodded. "And before I had the talk with him I called your father. My dad suggested it. Said your father would want to write up Lochinvar in his late Sunday morning edition."

"Oh," Ginny said, raising her eyebrows. "Now I get it. I won't get scolded for coming home after nine because nobody's home to scold me. Mother and Dad are at the Inn swooning over Lochinvar?"

John laughed. "That's right. I explained to your father that I'd be delayed coming back for you because I naturally wanted to talk to the manager and find out as much as I could about the new entertainer. Your dad said that under the circumstances it was all right as long as you got home before nine-thirty."

"Which it must be now," Ginny said, dropping her bike on the lawn and hurrying up the front steps. "Come in and have a glass of milk with me, John. What else did you find out about the glamorous superman?"

Back in the Gordons' kitchen, John said, "Nothing more about Lochinvar, but Mr. Crayne told me frankly that he wasn't going to encourage the teen-age crowd. He hopes Lochinvar will lure good-spenders from New York and all over Westchester County."

Ginny opened a box of chocolate cookies and poured milk into two tall glasses. "It doesn't matter," she said, perching on a stool across the kitchen table from John. "Mr. Crayne may not want our gang's fifty centses, but he'll get them anyway. Oh, dear, John, what on earth can we do?"

John forced himself to smile cheerfully. "All we can do is hang on and see what happens."

"But, John," Ginny wailed. "We've invested so much money in the Barn—almost five hundred dollars!"

Just then the phone rang. Ginny ran into the library to answer it.

"Ginny?" It was Lucy, her voice high-pitched with excitement. "Oh, Ginny, the most awful thing has happened."

"I know, I know," Ginny said drearily. "Lochinvar from out of the South. A dream man and the Pied Piper of Hamelin rolled into one superdooper—"

"But your own father," Lucy wailed. "Honestly, Ginny, can't you stop him?"

"What?" Ginny demanded. "Stop my father from doing what?"

"Writing him up on the front page of the *News!*" Lucy exploded.

"Oh, for heaven's sakes," Ginny said. "He's not

going to do that. Not unless Lochinvar has bitten a dog. There'll just be a line or two in the *Happenings* column."

"That's what you think," Lucy said sarcastically. "Your father just called my parents and told them to come right over to the Inn. He said he'd never heard anyone sing the *Kentucky Waltz* like that— that Lochinvar creature. Your father—your *own* father, Ginny, said he was so phenomenal he was going to write him up on the front page with pictures and everything."

"Oh, no," Ginny groaned. "If it had been anything but the *Kentucky Waltz!* Mother and Dad adore that song for some sentimental reason. I think Dad proposed while he and Mother were waltzing or something."

"Listen," Lucy hissed. "I've got a plan. But it all depends on whether or not laryngitis is catching! Is it?"

"I don't know," Ginny said. "But anyway, even if it is, Dad wouldn't catch it. He never even catches a cold with everyone in the whole house sneezing their heads off."

"I'm not talking about your father," Lucy yelled into the mouthpiece. "I'm talking about that awful man with the divine voice, which, if he had a good attack of laryngitis, wouldn't be so divine. And Joe Dakor has it. That's why he didn't come out to the opening this afternoon. He can hardly speak above a whisper. If only we could get those two together!"

"You've lost your mind," Ginny said emphatically. "In the first place I don't think laryngitis is catching. And, in the second place, if it is, Joe would be careful not to give it to anyone. He knows a lot about medicine, remember? He always wanted to be a surgeon—"

"Oh, all right," Lucy interrupted crossly. "Then you think of something. If that Lochinvar monster doesn't lose his voice soon, we've lost all our money."

"According to John," Ginny said calmly, "he's anything but a monster, unfortunately. No, Lucy, John and I have been all over it ever since he heard that man sing at dinner. There just isn't anything we can do except hope the high-school kids will keep on coming to the Barn because it's so much cheaper than the Inn."

"John!" Lucy cried impatiently. "Don't waste your time discussing the problem with *him!* He's so ethical and honorable and everything like that, he wouldn't let us try to do anything to the man, which *I* think we should do. He had no business coming to Harristown. There must be five billion other towns in New York State he could take himself and his old accordion to."

"Go to bed, Lucy," Ginny said. "You may not know it, but you're having a nervous breakdown. And the way I feel right now makes me sure that nervous breakdowns *are* catching."

CHAPTER THREE

BABS IN TROUBLE

Sure enough, there it was on the front page of the *Harristown News*. Ginny's parents were still asleep when she brought the Sunday paper in from the porch. Above a box on the lower half of the page was a picture of a tall, handsome, broad-shouldered man playing an accordion.

Ginny did not even bother to read the caption. "He must be really good," she reflected unhappily. "Otherwise, Dad wouldn't have played up the Inn's new attraction like this."

Lucy and Babs burst in through the front door then without even bothering to knock.

"Oh, oh, *OH*," Babs wailed. "We're absolutely ruined, Ginny. How could your father have done such a thing to us! Not a single solitary soul will come to the Barn for brunch today."

"Somebody will," Ginny said, suddenly remembering the envelope she had left locked in the cash box and had forgotten until this very minute.

"Who?" Lucy demanded. "There isn't anybody in town who is both blind and deaf."

Ginny laughed in spite of her inner worries. "Officer Bill will be there—at the Barn, I mean. When

37

he's on the eight to four a.m. shift he always eats brunch instead of breakfast and lunch."

"That's true," Lucy admitted. "But he'll go to the Grill for it. The Barn's too far away from the center of town."

Ginny shook her head. "Officer Bill promised me that he'd have brunch at our place every single Sunday—he and Mike, the Canton Building's janitor. They're great pals, you know. They promised to come out for afternoon snacks, too, on weekdays."

Lucy sniffed. "They're not patronizing us because they like our food, Ginny. Officer Bill just wants to keep an eye on you. He's afraid you'll get involved in another mystery."

"Anyway," Babs put in, "we can't make any money with only two steady customers. I've a good mind to bike out to the Inn now and smash that Lochinvar's accordion."

"Now listen, Babs," Ginny cautioned her soberly. "Get all such wacky notions out of your head right this minute. As John pointed out to me last night, that singer didn't come here deliberately to ruin our business. There's no sense in our wasting a lot of emotion in hating him."

Babs tossed her red-gold pigtails. "I don't care. I do hate him. And if you think I'm going to waste time helping you two make sandwiches today which nobody is going to eat, you've got another think coming."

"You certainly are going to help us," Lucy said briskly. "Honestly, the way you and Whiz calmly departed yesterday and left all those dishes for Ginny and me to do!"

Instantly Babs was contrite. "I'm awfully sorry. I thought about it after we got home. But I was so hungry! If only you'd let me eat one of those delicious, gooey cheeseburgers I kept taking to other people all afternoon!"

"Let's go," Ginny said. "It's almost nine and we open at ten." She took a light coat from the hall closet and threw it over her shoulders. "Another thing that worries me," she said as they biked toward the park, "is the heating problem. We're all right as long as this lovely hot weather lasts. But a cold snap is due soon. Then how will we heat the Barn?"

"Oh, oh," Lucy moaned. "Nobody ever thought of that."

"John did," Ginny told her. "Joe Dakor has some secondhand electric heaters for sale cheap which we'll have to buy eventually. But heating by electricity is pretty expensive."

"Don't let that worry you," Babs said. "We're not going to waste money heating an empty barn."

Ginny sighed. "Let's not give up so easily. How do you know? The place may be jammed again today." She thought for a minute and then added, "I'm pretty sure two men besides Officer Bill and Mike will show up for brunch today." Then she told them about Mr. Chadwell and the envelope he had left with her the night before.

"Oh, my goodness, Ginny," Lucy gasped. "You were crazy to get yourself into a situation like that. Five thousand dollars! Suppose that envelope isn't still in the cash box?"

"Of course it's still there," Ginny said firmly. "Why shouldn't it be?"

They got off their bikes and began to trundle them through the park. Lucy stared at Ginny and said, "You just got through telling us what you told John last night. That a tramp could easily break into the Barn. And once inside, it would be a simple matter to pry open the lock on the cash box—or simply walk off with the box itself."

"I know," Ginny admitted. "The reason why I left the envelope in the cash box instead of taking it home was because John pointed out to me that tramps seldom break into locked barns."

"Tramps," Babs added, "don't break into places at all. They don't like to do anything which might attract the attention of the police. That's because they can always be arrested and locked up in jail if they can't prove how they're earning their living. Officer Bill explained all that to me, Ginny, when we were trying to find out who stole your Great-Aunt Betsy's candlesticks from the Swap Shop."

"He explained it all to me, too," Lucy said. "The reason why we almost never have tramps in town is because the police always pick them right up on a vagrancy charge. After they spend a few days in jail they're ordered to leave town and never come back."

Ginny nodded. "John says tramps find out which towns to avoid through the hobo grapevine. So you see," she finished, "that's why I'm not worried about that envelope which is worth five thousand dollars to Mr. Henderson."

Lucy frowned thoughtfully. "But, Ginny," she protested. "The Barn isn't really in town."

"It just barely is," Babs corrected her. "The woods on the other side of the lane are in the next township, but the Barn itself is in Harristown. I know, because when Whiz was canvassing for the Boy Scouts, they told him that he shouldn't go to any house on the main road beyond Granny's."

"I don't know what you're both driving at," Ginny said, refusing to admit how worried she was about the envelope. "I know tramps traveling along the highway often sleep in those woods, but that doesn't mean one of them broke into the Barn last night and stole something which he had no way of knowing was there."

Lucy shrugged. "If John thinks it's okay to leave petty cash in the Barn all night I guess it's perfectly safe."

"We just can't worry about people breaking in," Ginny said. "Why, we've got about twelve dollars' worth of canned and bottled goods in there right now. If we had to carry all that home every night I'd give up."

"I give up anyway," Babs said morosely. "If you're smart, you'll carry that stuff to the grocery store on Monday and get your twelve dollars back."

Ginny squared her shoulders. "I won't do anything of the kind. We'll sell every bit of it. Wait and see."

The boys were already there when they arrived at the Barn. Whiz had put a hillbilly record on the Victrola and was listening to it with such a forlorn expression on his freckled face that Ginny burst out laughing.

"Oh, Whiz," she chuckled. "It's not as bad as that."

"It's worse," he said, without even looking up. "I heard that guy sing last night. What he doesn't do to the *Bubble Gum Polka*—"

"*You* heard him?" John demanded. "I didn't see you at the Inn last night."

"I didn't see you either," Whiz said sourly. "Nobody saw anybody but that gorgeous superman."

"Were you at the Inn last night, too?" Ginny asked Babs curiously.

Babs nodded. "I thought you knew. Your father called our parents from the Inn and asked them to join your parents there around nine. Mother knows how crazy we both are about hillbilly music so she said we could go with them and stay for half an hour or so."

"Half an hour was enough," Whiz said. "If anybody but us ever darkens this doorway again I'll eat my hat."

"Let's eat up all the perishables first," Babs said, peering into the refrigerator. "Oh, I forgot, there's nothing left."

Ginny briskly scrubbed her hands at the sink behind the sandwich counter. "There are plenty of delicious cheese spreads in these jars," she said. "And several loaves of bread. Come on, girls, let's get going."

"Aren't you going to see if that envelope is still in the cash box?" Lucy asked. "I'd like to see it. If it's worth five thousand dollars to Mr. Henderson we ought to frame it."

"What's worth five grand to whom?" Whiz asked as he turned off the Victrola.

Ginny explained. John was just as disapproving as she had anticipated. "Honestly, Ginny," he said. "How *do* you do it?"

"It ain't easy," Whiz said. "It takes years of practice. Ever since I can remember, Ginny has been getting herself involved in situations any normal person would—"

"Oh, stop it, Whiz," Ginny begged. "Mr. Henderson will show up soon and take the envelope away. And then Mr. Chadwell will come back for his money. There's really nothing involved about it at all. It's all very simple."

"I think you're mean to pick on her," Lucy cried, coming to the rescue of her best friend. "There's nothing wrong with Ginny except that she's generous and kind-hearted and—"

"Completely lacking in common sense," John finished for her. "The whole transaction doesn't make sense." He opened the cash box and stared at the envelope. "If this thing is worth five thousand bucks to Mr. Henderson, why didn't he show up yesterday? And why did Mr. Chadwell let you, Ginny, be responsible for collecting the cash for him?"

Ginny viciously pried the top off a jar of sandwich spread. "I don't know and I don't care," she said. "If I hadn't been so exhausted yesterday I would have refused to act as his—his—"

"Middleman," Whiz said. "John's right. There's something fishy about it, if you ask me."

"Nobody asked you," Ginny said crossly. Then she heard somebody coming up the lane. She whirled to look out the window. "Here come Officer Bill and Mike," she told the others. "And we haven't even a cup of coffee for them."

"I'll make some right away," Lucy said. "What else shall we give them, Ginny? Scrambled eggs and toast?"

"That's what we should give them," Ginny said. "But we used up every egg yesterday in the Western sandwiches. I should have brought some from home but my mind was so filled with Lochinvar I forgot."

"Never mind," John said, opening a can of corned beef hash. "If we fry slices of this and serve it with tomato catsup, they won't complain."

"That's right," Ginny said, inspecting the supplies in the cupboard. "I'll heat up this can of mushroom soup and add some mixed vegetables to it. That'll give them a nicely balanced meal."

"That takes care of them," Babs whispered as the two tall, broad-shouldered men came in the door. "But what if some other people show up?"

"We've tons of canned stuff," Ginny whispered back. "If you go home for some lettuce we can make a huge bowl of vegetable salad using John's famous salad dressing."

"All right," Babs agreed. "And I may as well buy some eggs at the delicatessen, too. Hard-boiled eggs in the salad would be nice." She took a dollar bill out of the cash box and, with a brief "hello" to Officer Bill and Mike, hurried past them to her bike.

"Hi, kids," the policeman said cheerily. "Got anything for us to eat? Mike and I figured the crowd here yesterday might have cleaned you out."

"It just about did," Ginny said with a grin. "But, if you don't mind waiting a few minutes, we'll serve you a delicious brunch."

"We're early," Mike said. "Don't rush. We had orange juice and a cup of coffee at the Grill before we left town." He strolled over to the Victrola and glanced at the record on the disk. "H-m-m. *Chime Bells.* I hear the Inn's got a new entertainer. A hillbilly singer."

"Don't mention his name around here, puhleeze," Whiz begged. "It affects us the way a red flag does a bull."

Officer Bill guffawed. "Afraid he'll steal all your customers, huh?"

"I wish you could pick him up on a vagrancy charge," Lucy said as she brought two bowls of thick, creamy soup from the counter to his table.

The big, burly policeman howled with laughter at that. He laughed so hard that tears streamed down his face.

Lucy stared at him. Even John looked surprised. They all knew that Officer Bill had a grand sense of humor but they had never seen him so convulsed with laughter before. Suddenly he sobered and wiped his face with his handkerchief. "You kids," he said in a choked voice, "you kids will be the death of me yet."

"I wish we could affect that Lochinvar man the same way," Ginny said sourly. "If thoughts could kill he'd be in his grave by now."

"It'll take a lot more than thoughts to kill that superman," Whiz said. "Have you seen him, Officer Bill?"

The policeman glared at him. "Now, when do I get time to go gallivanting out to the Inn?"

Officer Bill Roared With Laughter

"You must have seen his picture on the first page of this morning's *News*," Whiz said.

"That I did see," Officer Bill said. "Come on, Mike," he said to the janitor. "Eat your soup before it gets cold."

Mike ambled back from the Victrola and sat down at the table. "Soup at ten in the morning?" he asked, frowning. "I thought we'd have ham and eggs."

"Brunch," Ginny said hastily. "It should be a well-balanced meal."

He shrugged. "Never did care for vegetables."

"Then it's time you learned to like 'em," Officer Bill said crisply. "You'll never grow big and strong without lots of carrots and string beans."

Mike grinned. "Judging from the picture in the *News*, the Inn's new entertainer must have lived on carrots and beans. I thought those Kentucky mountaineers were skinny, half-starved people."

"You thought wrong," Officer Bill told him emphatically. "They're all as husky as oxen."

"Not according to the books I've read," Mike said stubbornly. "They all die of malnutrition at an early age."

"Those books," Officer Bill said, shaking his spoon at Mike, "were written before the State built the new roads. There are hardly any isolated mountain villages nowadays. And even though the soil is poor, the people grow and can plenty of vegetables for their families."

"Is that so?" Mike asked, raising his eyebrows. "Since when did you get so well-informed on Kentucky mountaineers?"

The policeman ignored the question and went on eating his soup. Mike ignored the soup.

"Oh, dear," Ginny thought. "The customer is always right. If only I'd remembered to bring some eggs from home!"

John came to the rescue. "If you don't like the soup, Mike," he said, "you can fill up on the corned beef hash the girls are frying. It's almost ready, isn't it, Ginny?"

"In half a sec," Ginny said.

"Now, that's more like it," Mike said when Lucy set the heaping plate in front of him. "And that coffee smells mighty good."

"I'll bring you a cup right away," Lucy said. "I hope you don't mind evaporated milk. We used up every bit of our cream yesterday."

"I don't exactly mind evaporated milk," Mike said, "but it seems to me that you kids could keep on hand simple things like eggs and cream."

Ginny's cheeks flamed. "You're absolutely right, Mike," she said, controlling her anger with an effort. "And after this we'll be sure to keep well-stocked."

"We didn't expect such a crowd yesterday," John said easily. "And with the weather so warm, we thought we'd sell a lot more cold drinks than tea and coffee."

"And cocoa," Lucy added. "I whipped so much cream yesterday my wrist still aches."

Mike grinned. "I'm not picking on you. This hash is as good as any I ever tasted."

"That it is," Officer Bill said. "And I for one prefer evaporated milk to cream."

They ate in silence after that while Ginny and Lucy made sandwiches. After Officer Bill and Mike left, Whiz said, "Those two are a riot, aren't they? I thought Officer Bill was really mad for a minute when they were arguing about Kentucky mountaineers."

"They're always arguing," John said, smiling. "If Bill says something is white, Mike insists it's black."

"I must say," Lucy put in, "that I thought Mike was right about the Kentucky mountaineers. I thought they ate nothing but acorns and were very puny."

Whiz hooted. "You girls never keep up with current events. Didn't you read about the Kentucky rural road program which is linking even the tiniest mountain settlements to the big cities? Pretty soon there won't be any hillbillies."

."I wish there weren't any now," Ginny said. "Is that Lochinvar an honest-to-goodness Kentuckian, or does he just sing in the dialect?"

"My guess is that he's the real McCoy," Whiz said. "Don't you agree, John?"

John nodded. "According to Mr. Crayne, he used

to be a wandering minstrel, straight from the hills."

"Used to be?" Ginny asked. "He didn't look very old in his picture."

"He's about thirty," John told her. "More or less."

Ginny stared out the window. "Not a soul in sight," she said discouragedly. "What on earth can be keeping Babs?"

"I," said Whiz, "am more interested in the arrival of your Mr. Henderson. I've never seen a thousand-dollar bill and never thought I'd see five of them all at the same time."

"What time is it, John?" Ginny asked. "I must remember to pick up my wrist watch at the jeweler's when I deposit our money in the bank on Monday."

"What money?" Whiz jeered.

"It's almost eleven," John said and added to Whiz, "We took in more than thirty-three dollars yesterday."

Whiz whistled shrilly through his fingers. "Gleeps, if it weren't for Lochinvar we might have doubled that today."

"We may yet," Ginny said without much hope. "All of our classmates said yesterday that they'd be back today."

But, an hour later, not one customer had appeared. "We might as well eat these sandwiches and drink the cocoa ourselves," Lucy said. "I'm famished. I didn't have anything but crackers and milk for breakfast."

"Let's not eat all of them," Ginny said. "Mr. Henderson and Mr. Chadwell are sure to show up soon." She came out from behind the counter and joined the others at one of the big tables in the middle of the room. "I hope they arrive at about the same time; then I won't have to have anything to do with the money."

"I don't think anyone will have anything to do with the money," Whiz said. "The whole thing was a figment of Mr. Chadwell's imagination, and he's an escaped lunatic who has already been returned to the insane asylum."

Ginny giggled. "He didn't look like a lunatic. He looked like a, well, a hard-boiled businessman."

"What do you mean, hard-boiled?" Lucy asked curiously.

"I don't know exactly," Ginny said. "He spoke very pleasantly, and all that, but there was something hard about him. I guess I mean cold-blooded. And he was so sure of himself."

"Speaking of lunatics," Whiz said, "what do you suppose happened to my wacky twin?"

"I can't imagine," Ginny said. "Buying the eggs and borrowing some lettuce shouldn't have taken more than half an hour."

"She probably broke the eggs and ate the lettuce," Whiz said. "She can't get near anything edible without eating it, and you know how clumsy she is with breakables."

"Babs isn't really clumsy," Ginny said. "She's just careless."

"It amounts to the same thing," Whiz said. "Which means that somewhere between here and Main Street a dozen eggs are lying in the gutter. She's scared to come back and tell us the bad news."

Ginny got up and walked restlessly to the door. Then she saw Babs pedaling furiously along the lane. "Here she comes," Ginny said. "And you're right, Whiz, her bike basket is empty."

"Oh, it's all too awful," Babs called breathlessly, coasting the rest of the way to the Barn. "Every single kid who goes to Junior-Senior High is at the Inn already."

"So that's where you've been," Whiz said, peering at her over Ginny's shoulder. "I thought you were sent for eggs and lettuce."

"I didn't bother," Babs said airily. "If you had gone to the Inn first as I did, you wouldn't have bothered either. It's packed and jammed. Even the tables on the porch were all filled by eleven o'clock."

Whiz groaned. "And they haven't even heard or seen him yet."

"They've seen him," Babs said. "He was just starting to sing when I left. I couldn't stand it. But I must admit if he wore cowboy clothes instead of dungarees and a checked shirt, he could double for a Western movie hero."

"Don't say it," Lucy moaned. "We know. Tall,

dark and handsome. And what he can't do with an accordion—"

"He won't do anything with an accordion today," Babs said mysteriously.

"Why not?" John asked.

"Never mind," Babs said evasively. "I'm starved. Let's eat up everything in the place and call it a day."

"Wa-it a minute." Whiz grabbed her arm and whirled her around to face him. "You've got that insane look in your eyes which spells TROUBLE. What have you been up to, dope?"

Babs pulled away from him. "I'm not a dope. The rest of you are idiots. I don't know how you can just sit here and let that fellow ruin our business. I, at least, did something to ruin *his* business."

Whiz grabbed his unruly red hair with both hands. "Oh, no," he groaned. "A thousand times no."

Ginny leaned weakly against the door. "The accordion," she gasped. "Oh, Babs, you—you didn't swipe it?"

CHAPTER FOUR

A THREAT

Babs tossed her red-gold pigtails. "I didn't swipe his old accordion," she told Ginny. "I simply put it someplace where it won't be easy to find."

"For that," Whiz said, shaking his head, "Officer Bill will put you someplace where it won't be easy for you to get out!"

"This is no time for joking," John said seriously.

"Who's joking?" Whiz demanded indignantly. "I always said she should have been taken straight from her playpen to reform school."

Suddenly Babs burst into tears. "I know I shouldn't have done it," she wailed. "But I simply couldn't resist it. There it was on the hall table and everyone else was in the dining-room or on the porch. The next thing I knew, I was running up the stairs with it."

"Stop bawling," Whiz ordered. "Where did you hide it?"

"The Wh-white Elephant," Babs sobbed. "You know. That room on the second floor Mr. Crayne almost never rents because it's so little and has only one tiny window in it. I don't think the maids even dust it except when it's rented. I put the accordion under the bed."

John collapsed on one of the wall benches, shaking with laughter. "Well, they can't put you in the pokey for that. Lochinvar happens to be occupying the White Elephant at the moment."

"Thank goodness," Ginny gasped, crumpling beside him. "One of the maids has probably found it by now. I was terrified for fear Babs had thrown it down the laundry chute."

"I wish I'd thought of that," Babs said defiantly. "I wish I'd thrown it in the furnace."

"I wish you'd been born with a brain," Whiz said in disgust. "Sometimes it's hard for me to believe our parents when they say we're twins."

Lucy giggled rather hysterically. "Nobody has to tell you you're twins, Whiz. Just look in the mirror."

"Thank you, no," Whiz said bitterly. "I don't wish to be reminded in any way of our unfortunate relationship."

"Oh, go dye your hair," Babs said crossly. "I don't like being related to you any more than you like being my brother."

John chuckled. "Cut it out, you two. You know you adore each other. But listen, Babs," he went on soberly. "No more of that stuff. Lochinvar may be a simple hillbilly, but if he ever decided to take the law into his own hands and give you a spanking, you'd eat standing up until Christmas vacation."

"I'm too old for spankings," Babs informed him

with a superior smile.

"Says you," Whiz put in. "I've a good mind to tell Lochinvar on you and stand by cheering while he wallops you."

"You know," Lucy said thoughtfully, "Babs may have something there."

"She's got too much there," Whiz said with a grin. "But it still hurts to get spanked."

"I don't mean that," Lucy said, laughing. "I mean maybe we should concentrate on doing something which may make Lochinvar so unhappy here that he'll leave town."

"Oh, *Lucy.*" Ginny got up and began to pace up and down. "Short of burning the Inn to the ground, what could we possibly do?"

"Don't put ideas in the little moron's head," Whiz cautioned.

"Get *all* such ideas out of all your heads," John said in a very serious tone of voice. He glanced at his wrist watch. "It's almost two, Ginny. I don't think your pals are going to show up."

"Oh," Babs cried. "I forgot about the envelope. What are you going to do with it, Ginny?"

Ginny sighed. "The rest of you can go home, but I've got to stay here until three. I sort of promised Mr. Chadwell. He said he'd drive out from New York as early today as he could."

"I keep telling you," Whiz began.

"Never mind the escaped lunatic angle," John interrupted. "Ginny's right. She's got to stay here until three. The rest of you can go home. I'll stay and keep her company."

"I'll stay, too," Lucy offered. "We can practice conjugating French verbs. John can be teacher."

"That's a good idea," Ginny said. "If we don't keep up with our homework, we won't be allowed to work here."

Whiz frowned at Babs who was gobbling sandwiches as fast as she could. "Seriously, gang," he said, "we might as well face it. This project is a flop. Do we try to stagger on for another week, or do we sell our equipment and try to retrieve some of our losses?"

"Don't be such a defeatist, Whiz," Ginny said. "The high-school crowd may not go for Lochinvar after all."

"Don't be such an optimist," he came back. "You forget that the guy is not cross-eyed and hasn't got two left feet. An atom bomb might keep our classmates away from the Inn, but I'm not quite up to making one."

"We should be able to do something to make him leave town," Lucy said. "Aren't Kentucky mountaineers supposed to be awfully superstitious?"

"They're supposed to be," Ginny said wearily. "But according to mastermind Reilly and Officer Bill all that is a thing of the past."

"Oh, some of them are probably still pretty superstitious," Whiz said. "But where does that get us?"

"Nowhere," John said firmly. "I want it strictly understood that Lochinvar is not to be annoyed in any way by any of us. He's got a perfect right to earn his living entertaining at the Inn."

"I just thought," Lucy said. "If he didn't get paid for singing week-ends, he'd be a vagrant, wouldn't he?"

"No, he wouldn't," John said with emphasis. "I should think that the way Officer Bill almost split his sides laughing when you presented that angle would have driven it out of your head."

"It *was* queer the way that struck him as being so hilariously funny, wasn't it?" Ginny asked.

The twins left and she went to the door to watch them pedal down the lane. The whole thing was really fantastic. They had started out so well, and now, overnight, the project was a flop. "Through no fault of our own," she said out loud.

"Say it in French," John ordered. "From now until three you girls are not to speak a word of English."

"*C'est si beau,*" Lucy sang.

"Don't sing," Ginny said in French. "It reminds me of that man."

At three o'clock she determinedly walked over to the cash box and took out the envelope. "I simply won't go through another night with this thing hanging over my head," she said to John. "What'll I do with it?"

"I think," John said slowly, "that under the circumstances you have every right to open it. Mr. Chadwell had no business giving you the responsibility of it in the first place. And since neither he nor Mr. Henderson has showed up—"

"I know what I'll do," Ginny cried impulsively. "I'll steam the flap open." She turned on the burner under the tea kettle.

"I don't think," Lucy said nervously, "that you ought to open other people's mail."

"It isn't *mail*," Ginny retorted. "I wish it were. In that case I'd simply turn it over to the postmaster."

"Oh, I see," Lucy said. "You want to find out the address of one of the men so you can return the envelope to them?"

"That's right," John said. "Ginny's responsibility ended at three o'clock. She has a perfect right to throw the envelope away since possessing it makes her jittery." He smiled. "But, as you pointed out, she's both kind-hearted and generous and so she's going to make an effort to find out who is the rightful owner of it."

In another minute Ginny had steamed the flap open. Gingerly she drew out the contents—five smaller, plain white envelopes—and laid them on the counter. Puzzled, she glanced up at John. "Now what?"

He grinned down at her. "As Whiz would say, the plot thickens. Aren't you going to see what's inside those envelopes?"

"Somehow, I don't like to," Ginny said with a frown. "It seems like prying."

"Prying?" Lucy demanded. "It seemed like prying to me when you steamed the flap open, but these envelopes aren't sealed. Since you've gone this far you may as well see what's in them. Maybe you'll find an address."

"Let's all do it," Ginny said. "Misery loves company."

So, simultaneously, they each opened an envelope and drew out a sheet of plain white paper. Then Lucy and Ginny opened the fourth and fifth envelopes. They, too, contained nothing but blank sheets of paper.

"Well, I never," Ginny cried in disgust. "Who would have thought that Whiz was right for once? Mr. Chadwell must have been an escaped lunatic after all!"

John thoughtfully examined each sheet of paper before he tucked them back in the envelopes. "I don't think he's a lunatic," he said, "although there's only a fine line between an idiot and a practical joker."

"Practical joker?" Ginny repeated, replacing the envelopes in the larger one. "But why on earth should a perfect stranger play a joke on me?"

"I have no idea," John said, smiling. "I don't indulge myself so I have no idea what makes practical jokers tick."

"Well, I have," Ginny said decisively. "And they don't play mean, silly tricks on people they never saw before in their lives." Without resealing the flap, she put the large envelope in the cash box and locked the box.

Lucy's blue eyes were round with surprise. "What on earth did you do that for, Ginny?" she asked. "Why lock up such perfectly worthless junk?"

Ginny shrugged. "Now that I know it's worthless I don't have to worry about it any more, but just in case one of those men shows up eventually I may as well keep it in a safe, handy place."

John arched his dark eyebrows. "Ginny, you don't really think that there is such a person as Henderson, do you?"

"Yes, I do," Ginny told him coolly. "There's something mysterious about all this. And I—"

"Oh, no," Lucy interrupted, collapsing in the nearest chair. "No, Ginny, not another mystery!"

John laughed. "This time she can indulge herself to her heart's content with my full approval. The chances of her crossing the path of a dangerous criminal in this case are practically nil." He started for the door. "I've got to scram. Promised Dad I'd help him clean the cellar."

Lucy gasped. "Oh, my goodness. That reminds

me. I told Mother I'd definitely be home at three-thirty." She hurried after John. "Coming with us, Ginny?"

"No," Ginny said absent-mindedly. "I want to stay here for a while—and think."

Without really seeing them, she stood at the door until they disappeared from view. Then she went back behind the counter and perched on the stool. Mr. Chadwell, she was sure, was not a practical joker. He had been coldly confident that a man named Henderson would give her five one-thousand-dollar bills for that envelope. He *might* have planned to play a practical joke on Henderson, but for some reason Henderson hadn't fallen into the trap. What had happened to him? And why hadn't Mr. Chadwell returned for the money he was so sure would be waiting for him here at the Snack Barn?

Suddenly the screen door opened. Ginny looked up. Standing on the threshold was a short, fat man who was wearing a very seedy-looking suit of clothes.

"Hello," he said in an unpleasantly hoarse voice, "I'm Henderson."

If he had smiled, Ginny's attitude might have been different. A smile might have disguised the furtive look in his small eyes. "How do you do, Mr. Henderson," she said, coldly polite.

He glanced over his shoulder twice as he shuffled from the doorway to the counter. "You got something for me," he whispered hoarsely. "Quick! Hand it over!"

Ginny stared at him appraisingly. She could see now that his suit was expensive and well made but had not been cleaned or pressed recently. Dried autumn leaves clung to the cuff of his trousers, and the elbows of his jacket were badly soiled. The collar of his bright pink shirt was crumpled, and the flashy tie that hung from it was a limp rag.

This Mr. Henderson, Ginny decided quickly, *is a natty dresser, but for some reason, he's grown careless. I'll bet those dusty shoes are usually so shiny you can see your face in them.*

"No stalling now, kid," his ragged voice broke into her thoughts. "Hand it over, and make it snappy!"

Ginny smiled briefly. This was not proceeding at all the way Mr. Chadwell had described the transaction. First Mr. Henderson was to give her five one-thousand-dollar bills, and then she was to hand over the envelope.

"I'm not stalling," she said calmly. "I'm simply waiting for you to identify yourself."

"Iden—" He stopped and glanced over his shoulder for the third time. "Listen, pigeon," he said, his voice grating, "a guy named Chadwell left an envelope with you, which envelope you're supposed to hand over to me—Henderson. I'm Henderson. That's all the identification you need."

Ginny shrugged. The contents of the envelope were worthless, but she had no intention of letting this disagreeable little man know that. "I'm sorry," she said, slipping off the stool. "Mr. Chadwell told me that you were to identify yourself by giving me five one-thousand-dollar bills. If you don't, I can't give you the envelope." She moved down the counter and carefully inspected the wax-paper wrappings on the leftover sandwiches.

"These will keep very nicely in the refrigerator," she muttered to herself, deliberately giving the impression that she had dismissed the man from her mind.

She heard him shuffling behind her on the other side of the counter. There was something ominous about his silence as he followed her. Suddenly Ginny realized that Henderson knew he could force her to give him the envelope without giving her anything in exchange.

If she screamed for help no one would hear her. The nearest house was old Mrs. Blaketon's, half a mile away. Even if the little old lady and her maid heard a scream, what could they do? Not far from the big stone house was the gardener's cottage which young Dr. and Mrs. Bascom had rented from Mrs. Blaketon. Could they hear her if she screamed?

No, Ginny decided, as she opened the refrigerator and put the sandwiches inside. *Besides, the Bascoms aren't home. They love hillbilly music, too. They're at the Inn.*

Dozens of cars were whizzing along the main highway at the other end of the lane, but the sound of their motors would drown out her cries for help. Thinking fast, Ginny opened the cupboard and pretended to be absorbed completely in taking a mental inventory of the cans and jars.

Now she really was stalling for time. The smart— or rather, *wise*—thing to do, of course, was to get rid of Henderson by giving him the worthless envelope. Even if it developed later that the man wasn't Henderson, no harm would have been done. No one could blame her for giving away what amounted to nothing in exchange for nothing.

"I've been counting," the hoarse voice behind her said. "Counting to ten. Slowly. I just got to eight. When I get to ten, sister, you'd better give me that envelope—or else."

CHAPTER FIVE

A HIDDEN WEAPON

"Eight," the ragged voice behind Ginny repeated. "Ny-un."

Ginny moved swiftly down the counter to the mirror. One glance at the fat man's reflection told her that he meant business. His small eyes were mere slits, and his pudgy hands were clenched into fists.

On the counter not three feet from him was the cash box with the key in the lock. He must have seen it when he came in. All he had to do was turn the key, lift the lid, take the envelope, and shuffle out of the Barn. There was nothing she could do to stop him. Unless—unless—

Ginny was quite sure that the man was stronger than she, but she was equally sure that she could run faster than he could. The cash box was not heavy now, for John had taken most of the money out of it the night before.

"Ten," the hoarse voice rasped.

To think was to act with Ginny. She ducked under the counter, grabbed the box and sprinted for the door. But the fat man, in spite of his weight, was surprisingly agile. And he had a head start, for he began to move the moment Ginny ducked under the counter. He reached the door a split second ahead of her and stood there blocking the way when she skidded to a stop.

"I don't like to get rough with dames," he said hoarsely. "I gave you a chance to give me that envelope. Now I'm gonna take it away from you."

And then Ginny heard someone biking along the lane. "I wouldn't get rough with anyone," she said, keeping a firm grip on the box. "Someone's coming. And it's probably Officer Bill. He's one of our best customers, you know."

As though she had spoken words of magic, the man lumbered through the door and disappeared in the woods. Not until that moment did Ginny realize how frightened she had been. Her knees were shaking when she returned the cash box to the counter, and she quickly sat down in the nearest chair.

When John came in she looked up at him gratefully and said, "Boy, oh, boy, am I ever glad you came back!"

He stared at her. "Why, Ginny, you're as white as a sheet. What happened?"

"Henderson," she told him. "At least he said he was Henderson. He came for the envelope, but I wouldn't give it to him."

"Why not?" John demanded. "For Pete's sake, Ginny, I thought you were dying to get rid of the thing."

Ginny sighed. "I suppose I was a dope, but, John,

he refused to give me the money first, and he acted so shifty, always looking over one shoulder. And then he said I'd better give it to him, or else. That did it." She laughed rather shakily. "You know me, John. If he'd asked me for it nicely I probably would have given it to him, because after all, what's in the envelope isn't worth five thousand dollars to anyone."

John smoothed his hair back from his forehead. His eyes were dark with anger. "So he threatened you?" he asked slowly.

Ginny nodded. "If you hadn't come when you did—" She stopped and stared at him. "By the way, what made you come back?"

John smiled fleetingly. "Lochinvar," he said. "When I got home I found a note from Dad saying that instead of cleaning the cellar he had taken Mother to the Inn for tea. He invited you and me to join them there, so I came back for you."

Ginny shook her head sadly. "That man must be positively hypnotic. I can't believe that opera-lovers like your parents, John—"

"Never mind about that," John interrupted. "Let's get back to Henderson. If he threatened you, we should tell Officer Bill the whole story at once."

"Don't be ridic, John," Ginny said briskly. "He would only laugh his head off at us. None of it makes any sense. Remember how convulsed he was when Lucy suggested that he pick up Lochinvar on a vagrancy charge?"

John thought for a moment. "It would sound pretty silly to Bill. If he believed any of it, he'd say that both men were simply making you the victim of a practical joke."

"If there were anything of value in the envelope," Ginny went on, "we'd have something to show Officer Bill. But how on earth can we get him interested in five blank envelopes containing nothing but five blank sheets of paper?"

"We can't," John agreed. "About all we can do is make sure that none of you girls is ever left here alone again. I hope I'm here when that guy comes back."

"I don't think he'll come back," Ginny said. "I think he'll get in touch with Chadwell. Right away. And Chadwell will tell him that he made a mistake —that he gave me the wrong envelope. And then the two men will make arrangements to meet someplace else. Because, John, Chadwell must have made a mistake."

"That would explain a lot of things," John said. He followed Ginny outside after they had locked the windows and snapped the padlock on the door. "It would explain why Chadwell probably didn't come back today. If he gave you the wrong envelope he'd know that there wouldn't be any five thousand bucks waiting for him here."

Ginny nodded and picked up her bike. "One

thing it doesn't explain is why Henderson didn't give me the money. He obviously thought the envelope contained what he wanted; otherwise he wouldn't have tried so hard to get it."

"Maybe you got the deal mixed up," John said as they biked along the lane. "Maybe the deal was that Henderson was to examine the contents of the envelope before he gave you the money. That makes more sense than the other way round."

"I didn't get it mixed up," Ginny said. "But I must say I can't blame Henderson for wanting to see what he was getting before he paid me for it."

"I can't blame him for that myself," John admitted. "I wish you'd given him the envelope, then that would have been the end of the whole thing." He shook his head. "Any other girl in the world would have done that. If you had more sense and less courage, life would be a lot simpler."

Ginny laughed. "That's a left-handed compliment, John Blaketon."

"I didn't mean it as a compliment," John said, grinning. "Shall we bike on out to the Inn? If we don't, you'll be the only girl in school tomorrow who isn't swooning over Lochinvar."

"I have no intention of swooning over him," Ginny said tartly. "But I must confess I'd like to see and hear him."

As they biked past the Reillys' home, Whiz called out from the porch glider, "Ha, ha, ha, Ginny! And a couple of ho-ho's. Next time I tell you you're playing games with a lunatic, I guess you'll believe me."

Ginny got off her bike and stared up at him. "What are you talking about?"

Whiz yawned and stretched. "John told me what you found in the envelope. Five blank envelopes containing blank sheets of paper. Ha, ha, ha! Ho, ho, ho!"

"Ha, ho, yourself," Ginny said, sinking down on the steps. "You tell him, John. Then he'll sing another tune."

Whiz sat up. "Don't use that word, sing, around me—or the word, tune. What cooks, John?"

John joined him in the glider as he told him that Henderson had called for the envelope and had threatened Ginny. "From now on," he finished, "the girls are not to go out to the Barn unless one of us is with them."

"Gleeps," Whiz shouted. "The thing makes sense now."

Ginny rested her elbows on her knees and cupped her chin in her hands. "Sense to the senseless, but not to me."

Whiz looked genuinely surprised. "Do you mean to tell me that a famous detective like you hasn't figured it out?"

"I figured out that Mr. Chadwell must have given me the wrong envelope," Ginny said. "If that's what you mean."

Whiz shook his head. "People don't put blank sheets of paper into envelopes for nothing. No, mastermind, if Henderson was so anxious to get the envelope away from you, the contents must be valuable. Therefore, there must be invisible writing on those so-called blank sheets of paper."

Ginny jumped to her feet. "Why, Whiz Reilly," she cried, "you're a genius! Have you still got that chemistry set you bought ages ago when we thought poor old Mr. Shultze was a German spy?"

Whiz nodded. "I have, and if there's invisible writing on anything, one of the solutions will bring it to light."

"Is it as good as all that?" John asked dubiously.

"It should be," Whiz told him. "It cost me a buck and about twenty cereal box tops. According to the ad in the Sunday comics, it is only surpassed by chemicals FBI scientists use in the big technical lab in Washington." He slid off the glider and started for the front door.

"Wait a minute," John said. "Ginny and I were due at the Inn ten minutes ago, so we can't go back to the Barn with you. Here's my key to the padlock."

"And here," Ginny said, reaching into the pocket of her skirt, "is my key to the petty cash box. Are you going to experiment out there, Whiz, or bring the papers back here to your room?"

"I'll bring the papers back here," Whiz said promptly, "and lock myself in my room. Then maybe Mother and Dad will think I'm doing my math homework."

John glared at him sternly. "Haven't you done your homework yet, Whiz? You know the rule Aunt Barbara laid down about you twins. If you don't keep up in school you won't be allowed to wait on tables."

Whiz grinned. "I haven't done my homework, John, because I can't. And neither can Babs. There are five problems and they simply don't make sense."

"They would," Ginny told him severely, "if you stayed awake in math class."

"I stay awake all right," Whiz retorted. "But that new math instructor has the erroneous impression that we were taught algebra in the seventh grade. He keeps mumbling and muttering about unknown quantities he refers to as x. As far as I'm concerned, x is the right answer to all five problems." He disappeared into the house, slamming the door behind him.

"The twins," Ginny said to John as they biked on toward the center of town, "are not what you'd call human adding machines."

"And you are," John said, his dark-blue eyes twinkling, "so I guess you'll have to help them with their math homework if we're going to stay in business."

"If," Ginny said with a sigh. "Oh, John, I'm really very upset about it all. We've invested so much money in the Barn. Half of me can't help siding with Babs and Lucy. Maybe we ought to do something to make Lochinvar leave town."

They rode along in silence until they reached the Inn which was about a quarter of a mile from where Orchard Street crossed Main. The terraced lawns sloped down to the street and the borders were bright with riotously blooming dahlias and chrysanthemums.

Ginny and John turned their bikes over to an attendant who gave them each a check to correspond with the one he looped over their handlebars. "Keep telling the manager," he mumbled, "we gotta have another bicycle stand. Gotta have about four more bike stands. And I gotta have an assistant." He shook his head worriedly. "Packed and jammed with kids, the Inn is, now that that Lochinvar wanders around singing."

"I wish he'd wander out to the Barn," Ginny said crossly. And then she saw him. The tall, broad-shouldered entertainer was perched on the porch railing, surrounded by an admiring group of boys and girls. As Ginny glanced up at him, frowning, he glanced down at her, grinning. It was such a friendly grin that she stopped hating him from that moment on.

"Why, he-he—" Ginny stuttered, "why, John, he looks just the way you're going to look when you stop growing! And I'll bet he's just as nice as he is nice looking.''

Several of their classmates called to them. "Hi, Ginny." "Hi, John."

As agilely as a cat, Lochinvar vaulted over the railing, neatly cleared the flower beds, and landed lightly on the slope not two feet from Ginny. He held out his hand to her.

"Welcome, stranger," he said. "I bin a-pinen to meet you, Miss Gordon. Met your paw last night, and a mighty civil man-person he is."

His soft southern drawl won Ginny over completely. There was the rhythm of poetry in his simple sentences, and she could easily guess now why he had been such an overnight success.

"Hello, Mr. Lochinvar," she said, smiling up at him. "I've heard an awful lot about you."

He shook hands with John then and said, "Are you-all a-goen to drap in fer a leetle? We-all are haven a singen party and we'd be mighty proud if you'd jine us."

"My parents," John told him, "are waiting for us at a table in the tea-room. At least, I don't see them on the porch."

Lochinvar tucked Ginny's hand through the crook of his arm. "A witch er the devil," he said, "tuck off with my accordion, but you kin accompany me on the pianny, I'll be bound."

"Oh," Ginny gasped. "Haven't you found it yet? It's—" She stopped herself just in time.

"I Bin A-Pinen to Meet You, Miss Gordon."

The handsome singer's voice was blank with amazement. "Hit's whar, Miss Ginny?" he asked. "I heered tell you is a might knowen detective, and I'd be plumb grateful if you'd holp me find hit."

Ginny bit her lip. "I heard you'd lost it," she said slowly. "And I was just wondering if you'd searched your room carefully."

"We'll both help you search," John offered. "Mr. Crayne hires extra help over the week-ends, you know. Young girls who aren't really experienced maids. Perhaps one of them put your accordion in what she thought was a good safe place." He winked at Ginny significantly.

She bit her lip again, this time to keep from laughing. A young girl *had* put the accordion in what she thought was a good safe place. That Babs!

"I'm plumb tuckered out with sarchin'," Lochinvar said as they followed him up the steps to the porch. "But I didn't sarch my own room." He led the way through the laughing crowd of young people, and Ginny and John followed him up the stairs to the second floor.

The door to the White Elephant was slightly ajar, Ginny noticed, and wondered if it was Babs or one of the maids who had forgotten to close it. "Most of the Inn's guests," she told Lochinvar as he strode down the hall ahead of them, "lock their doors when they go out and leave the key at the front desk downstairs."

"I niver locked a door in my life," the man said. "Down home there hain't no needcessity fer hit." He put his hand on the knob, and then it happened. Water deluged him from head to foot and a bucket crashed to the floor.

Lochinvar instinctively covered his face with his left arm, and Ginny saw something that made her eyes pop open with amazement. Under his thick woolen jack-shirt, the man carried a pistol in a shoulder holster! With his left arm raised, and his shirt front drenched with water, the outline of the gun's handle stood out plainly.

Ginny was so surprised for a minute she couldn't move. Lochinvar left his door unlocked, but carried a pistol in a shoulder holster!

It didn't make sense.

CHAPTER SIX

A BROKEN WINDOW

Before Ginny could recover from her surprise, John had dashed across the hall to the rest room and he came back with an armful of towels. Together they helped the spluttering entertainer mop up the water which had cascaded down upon him when he opened the door.

"Wh-what happened?" he demanded, grinning. "A booby trap?"

John nodded. "Some fool put that bucketful of water on top of the door. It balanced there until you touched the knob."

Lochinvar shook his head in bewilderment. "A man gone daft, most likely," he said. "I'll beat him haf to death when I cotch him. Spilen my nice new boughten cloes!"

"Oh, they're not spoiled," Ginny assured him. "But you'd better change right away. You don't want to catch a cold."

John's eyes twinkled and Ginny knew what he was thinking. Nothing would please Lucy and Babs more than the news that Lochinvar might catch a cold. The entertainer's sharp black eyes caught the amused look on her face and he asked suspiciously,

"Hev you an idee who could o' set that thar booby trap?"

"You'd better change right away," Ginny repeated hastily. "John and I'll wait downstairs. If you want us to help you look for the accordion we'll come back."

Ten minutes later Lochinvar came down. He was wearing a gay plaid shirt that was obviously as brand new as his dungarees. Folded against one hip was the missing accordion. He strode across the crowded tea-room to the table where Ginny and John were sitting with Mr. and Mrs. Blaketon.

"I found hit," he said, grinning. "Right onder my bed. I niver would o' thought o' looken thar iffen you hadn't put me up to hit."

He began to sing and play then, the *Bubble Gum Polka,* and Ginny was so enthralled she completely forgot to worry about the fate of the Snack Barn.

That evening at dinner her father said, "So you think I was right to feature Lochinvar on the front page of the *News* today?"

Ginny nodded. "He's simply super, Dad. I can't see why he wastes his time in this little suburb."

"I doubt if he'll be here long," Mr. Gordon said. "Some talent scout will pick him up soon."

"I hope so," Ginny said. "He's ruined our business."

"That's a shame," Mrs. Gordon said sympathetically. "And you did so well on the opening day.

Perhaps the older crowd will keep coming to the Barn even if your classmates don't."

"They won't," Ginny said discouragedly. "It's too long a walk from where they park their cars, and if we get any rain the lane will be muddy as anything. Besides," she went on forlornly, "the whole idea was to have a place where the Junior-Senior High crowd could get together after school and week-ends. We hoped eventually that it might develop into a community project if we ran it under adult supervision. You know, something like the Police Athletic League. Harristown hasn't a PAL, but it should."

"It certainly should," her father said soberly. "Teen-agers are apt to get into mischief unless they have something definite to do in their spare time." He leaned across the table to pat Ginny's hand. "Don't give up, honey," he said. "I have a feeling Lochinvar will be in Hollywood by Christmas."

"We can't hold out till then," Ginny said. "We'll have to heat the place any day now. And the two secondhand heaters Joe Dakor is reserving for us in the Swap Shop will use up every bit of the capital we have left. Not to mention the fact," she said bitterly, "that heating by electricity is expensive."

"The same old bugaboo, the electric company's bill," Mr. Gordon said, smiling. "That almost threw you when you launched the Swap Shop, didn't it?"

"That's right," Ginny said unhappily. "The worst part of the mess we're in right now is that we can't ask Joe to reserve those heaters for us much longer. When the first cold snap comes he'll be able to sell them to someone else. Then that means that even if Lochinvar left town we couldn't keep the Barn open."

"You *are* in a predicament," Mrs. Gordon said. "And heating by kerosene is cheap but rather dangerous. Otherwise, I'd let you have the two kerosene stoves we have in the garage."

Ginny shook her head. "Officer Bill would have a fit. We have to be very careful not to create a fire hazard. And as for the Public Health laws, why, those screens we had to tack over the windows to keep out flies cost us a small fortune."

"I can sympathize with your problems," her father said, pushing back his chair. "I can remember when I first started the *News*, I was appalled at the rapidity with which my capital disappeared."

Ginny followed her parents into the living-room. "I guess we might as well give up," she said, gathering her schoolbooks.

"You mean sell your equipment?" her father asked. "And try to recoup your losses?"

"Oh, I hate to have you do that," Mrs. Gordon said as she picked up her knitting. "Joe could easily dispose of the stove and the refrigerator and the Victrola for you at a profit, I imagine. But the furniture and the counters—I can't think of anyone who would want them. And John worked so hard."

"He certainly did," Ginny agreed. "And we spent an awful lot of money on plumbing and having the place wired, none of which we can hope to get back if we go out of business."

Mr. Gordon folded his hands behind his back and began to pace up and down. "I'm almost sorry now I gave the Inn so much publicity."

"I've thought about that, Dad," Ginny said, trying to sound cheerful. "John and I think that it was probably all for the best. Some big theatrical agency may see your write-up of Lochinvar. John says they subscribe to lots of small-town papers. And Lochinvar couldn't be more photogenic."

Mrs. Gordon smiled. "He certainly is. Well, Ginny, let's be optimistic. Keep open another week. Maybe Lochinvar will be lured to Hollywood before really cold weather sets in."

All the next day in school Ginny could hardly keep her mind on her lessons. She tried to concentrate on French verbs, but conjugating them seemed unimportant compared to the fate of the Snack Barn. And she was scolded twice for inattention in her favorite classes, math and bookkeeping. At last the long school day dragged to an end.

Ginny met the other Hustlers at the bike stand by the long front steps. "No soap," Whiz said without any preliminary greeting. "I tried every known chemical formula on those sheets of paper, and whatever is on them, if anything, is still invisible."

"I hope you didn't ruin them," Ginny said worriedly. "Do they look as though you'd been fooling with them?"

Whiz pursed his lips and glared at her through narrowed green eyes. "I'll have you know, madam," he said loftily, "that even the FBI experts couldn't guess that I'd tested them."

"That's an idea," Babs said. "Let's send them to the FBI lab in Washington. Maybe those experts can figure out why Henderson thinks they're so valuable."

Whiz howled with raucous laughter. "I'm afraid, lame-brain," he said, "that G-men have other more important things to do."

Ginny was staring at his twin. "By the way, Babs Reilly," she said. "Did you set up that booby trap on Lochinvar's door?"

Babs turned pale beneath her freckles. "H-How d-did you know about that?" she stammered.

"Because," John put in, "we were with him when he all but drowned." He shook his finger under Babs's snub nose. "After we bawled you out for swiping the man's accordion did you have the nerve to go back and—"

"I went back to get his old accordion," Babs interrupted tearfully. "I was going to bring it downstairs to him, but then, right outside the White Elephant I saw a step ladder and a bucket of clean water. One of the Inn's janitors must have been on the verge of cleaning the marble staircase when he was called away. Anyway, I—I—"

"Couldn't resist the temptation," John finished for her. "For Pete's sake, Babs, will you ever grow up? If Lochinvar had been wearing an expensive suit of clothes it might have been ruined. And, frankly, if he'd been wearing anything but a shirt and dungarees which water can't harm, I'd have had to tell him who I suspected was responsible."

"I almost told him anyway," Ginny told Babs sternly. "He's a swell person and was a very good sport about it all. Anybody else would have complained to the management, and if Mr. Crayne had investigated, he might well have found out that you were lurking around the halls yesterday."

"Oh, Ginny," Babs wailed. "The housekeeper saw me when I sneaked down the stairs. She was just coming out of the linen room after I— Oh, oh! How do you know Lochinvar didn't report it to the manager?"

"I don't know," Ginny said. "But I'm pretty sure he thinks a kid had something to do with both pranks. And he didn't strike me as the kind of guy who'd tattle on kids. Don't you agree, John?"

John nodded. "Actually, I think he suspects you and me, Ginny. It was all too, too pat. The way we suggested that he search his room just then." He grinned. "As you pointed out yesterday, practical

jokers usually like to be around to witness the suf-
ferings of their victims."

"True, too true," Ginny said bitterly. "That's
why I couldn't believe Mr. Chadwell was playing a
practical joke on me when he gave me that envelope." She turned to Whiz. "By the way, where is
it now?"

For answer, Whiz handed her the little key to the
petty cash box. "In the exact spot where I found it,"
he said. "I biked out to the Barn last evening after
I'd dried the papers and returned them to their
original pristine whiteness. In fact," he admitted
ruefully, "I'm such a creature of habit, I resealed
the envelope. Hope you don't mind."

"I couldn't care less," Ginny said. "Sealed or un-
sealed, it means nothing to me."

"Nothing means anything to me," Lucy complained. "I don't know what any of you are talking
about. Booby traps and the FBI lab! What *has* happened since I left you yesterday afternoon?"

"I'll explain while we ride out to the Barn,"
Ginny said, straddling her bike. "I would have told
you at lunch but I didn't go to the cafeteria today.
I went home instead. Mother had to go to a meeting
of the Women's Exchange, and Lila's home with a
cold. So I had to fix up something for Dad. If I'd
known in advance," she finished, "I'd have brought
home some of the leftover sandwiches which I put
in the Barn's refrigerator yesterday while Hender-

son was there."

"Yummy-yum," Babs said, "let's bike out and eat them now. I'm starved."

"That's not news," Whiz said. "When the sun dawns on your loss of appetite Ginny's father will write it up on the front page."

Babs tossed her carroty pigtails. "As a matter of fact, I'm not going to the Barn. I'm going to Granny's. Monday is Riba's baking day. I'd rather have a hunk of chocolate-marshmallow cake than old dried-out sandwiches."

"I'm with you there," Whiz said. "Let's go."

Lucy watched them ride off. "Honestly," she said in exasperation. "Those two are about as much help as cockroaches."

"Not as much," John said as the three of them pedaled toward Main Street. "Roaches and ants would at least help us eat up the stuff we'll never be able to sell."

They rode along in depressed silence until they had almost reached the Barn. Then Ginny called to John who was riding ahead of the girls, "Oh, gosh, I left my key to the padlock in the pocket of the skirt I wore yesterday, and Whiz has yours."

John jumped off his bike. "I'll ride back to Granny's and get my key from Whiz. It won't take long."

"*If* he has it with him," Ginny said. "He probably left it in the pocket of the jeans he wore yesterday." She let out a tired sigh. "Oh, let's all go home. If Lucy and I have to stand around waiting while you bike all the way in to the Reillys' and back—"

"That won't be necessary," John interrupted suddenly in a strangely tense voice. "Look, Ginny."

Ginny braked to a stop beside him and followed the direction of his pointing finger. "Oh, oh," she groaned. "Someone's ripped one of our brand new screens off that window."

"Ginny," Lucy gasped as she joined them. "Who could have done such a mean, mean thing to us?"

"That isn't all," John said, hurrying on toward the Barn. "The same mean someone smashed every bit of the glass in the window frame." He climbed over the sill and said from inside, "There's no doubt about it, girls, someone broke into the Barn last night. The hinges have been pried off the petty cash box."

Ginny scrambled in through the broken window and Lucy followed her in another minute. The lid was still on the cash box, but the battered hinges hung from the bottom bolts. Ginny darted over to the counter and snatched off the lid.

"John," she got out. "The envelope is gone!"

CHAPTER SEVEN

MORE BAD NEWS

John and Lucy hurried to peer over Ginny's shoulder. There was no sign of the big white envelope Mr. Chadwell had given her on Saturday.

"This is too much," Ginny said. "Help me count the money so we can find out how much has been stolen. I'm surprised there's any left at all."

They worked in silence until John said, "Twenty nickels, Ginny."

"Six quarters and ten dimes," she said, after checking Lucy's pile of coin. "And three fifty-cent pieces. Umm. Five dollars. Which is exactly what we left in the box yesterday, John."

He nodded. "It's baffling. I can't imagine why whoever broke in didn't take it, too."

"I can," Ginny said. "Five dollars is a mere drop in the bucket to Henderson. According to Mr. Chadwell he was supposed to give me five *thousand* dollars for that silly envelope."

"Oh," Lucy gasped, "then you think it was Mr. Henderson who broke into the Barn last night?"

"I'm sure of it," Ginny said. "Who else would want that envelope? He knew it was in the box because I grabbed it off the counter yesterday and tried to run off with it when he threatened me."

"For heaven's sakes," Lucy moaned, "please bring me up to date on what happened to you."

"First," Ginny said, "let's check up on the left-over sandwiches. If they're too stale we'll have to make fresh ones. Officer Bill may show up any minute for a snack." She opened the refrigerator door, and then whirled around to face Lucy and John. "Well, I like that! Whiz must have had a feast when he brought the envelope back here last evening. There's not one sandwich left."

"Those Reillys," Lucy said, hurrying to look into the refrigerator. "Honestly, all they think about is food!"

"That's not exactly true," John said mildly. "Whiz worked like the dickens before we opened. And I guess we can't begrudge him a little food every now and then. Aunt Barbara often serves only a light supper Sunday nights, so Whiz was probably starved by the time he biked out here, and he must have figured that the sandwiches wouldn't keep."

Ginny sniffed. "You know very well Mrs. Reilly's light suppers amount to a big, satisfying meal. Macaroni and cheese with salad, pie and cocoa isn't exactly a starvation diet." She climbed up on the stool behind the counter. "Now we're in a real jam. Officer Bill was a good sport about that peculiar brunch we gave him yesterday, so we must make up for it today. Nobody thought to bring any fresh loaves of bread."

"I'll bike back to town for some," John offered. "Shall I get eggs and lettuce and milk, too?"

"And cream," Lucy reminded him. "If Mike shows up with Officer Bill he'll surely want a cup of coffee. With *cream*, remember?"

John laughed good-naturedly. "I'd better fix up a trailer for my bike." He started for the door.

"Wait a minute, John," Ginny said. "Lucy and I had better go in for the food. You've just got to fix that screen before Officer Bill shows up."

John stared at her. "Why? It's evidence of breaking and entering."

"It's also," Ginny pointed out, "a violation of the Public Health laws. Besides, we aren't going to give Officer Bill any evidence. We aren't going to tell him a thing."

"Oh, yes, we are," John said firmly. "That fat little man threatened you yesterday and then he broke into the Barn. Now that we have proof—"

"We haven't any real proof," Ginny said emphatically. "I'll bet if the matter were taken to court, Henderson would get off scot-free. When you get right down to it, all he did was break in to get something which was his and which I had refused to turn over to him. His word," she went on, "is as good as mine. He could argue that the arrangement between him and Chadwell was that I was first to give him the envelope and *then* he was to give me the money. You said yourself, John, that it makes more sense that way."

"True, true," John admitted. "But Henderson had no business taking the law into his own hands. If he felt he had a legal right to that envelope, all he had to do was notify Officer Bill that you—"

"Henderson," Ginny interrupted, "does not care for the police. At least, that's the impression he gave me. When I mentioned Officer Bill's name, he faded into the woods like a pale ghost."

"Ghost," Lucy cried. "That's it."

Ginny turned to her. "That's what, Lucy Tryon? Don't tell me you think a ghost ripped off our screen and pried open our cash box?"

Lucy flushed. "No, I don't. I was just thinking out loud. Pay me no mind."

"I certainly won't," Ginny retorted tartly. "Not if you're thinking about ghosts." She grinned. "Start the coffee, please, and I'll make a list of what we need. We've simply got to be more businesslike."

John had climbed out of the broken window and was examining the screen. "I can fix this in a jiffy, Ginny," he said. "And when Whiz shows up, I'll send him to the glazier's for a piece of glass and some putty. But I still think it's high time the police were told about your little man."

"Why must you be so stubborn, John?" Ginny demanded crossly. "If the police are notified, one of Dad's reporters will hear about it and then my goose is cooked. Right now Mother and Dad are all for the Snack Barn and they're both sorry that Lochinvar is ruining our business. But if there's even a hint of anything mysterious going on, Mother's attitude will change for the worse."

John grinned. "All right, you twisted my arm, Ginny. Besides, now that Henderson has his envelope, we've probably seen the last of him."

"Of course we have," Ginny said emphatically. "And as for Chadwell, if he comes back for his money, I'll simply tell him the truth. Then he can notify the police if he wants to, which I very much doubt."

"Why?" John asked curiously. "Chadwell has obviously just been done out of five grand."

"I know," Ginny admitted. "But, if you ask me, I don't think either of them wants to have anything to do with the police. The very fact that they picked this place for the rendezvous makes me feel sure that it wasn't an open-and-above-board business transaction in the first place. Why didn't they arrange to meet at the Inn?"

"That's right," Lucy said, measuring coffee into the coffee maker. "Why didn't they?"

John climbed back in through the window and took a hammer and some tacks from the tool chest under one of the wall benches. "We can't waste time wondering about what makes them tick. You girls had better get going. It's after four."

Ginny pushed back the cuff of her sweater. "So it is. My, it's nice to have my wrist watch back. I was lost without it. Oh, that reminds me." She climbed out of the window and picked up the algebra book she had left in her bike basket. Tucked between the pages was the pass book she had taken to the bank at noon. She waved it through the window at John. "Where'll I keep things like this now that our cash box is about as safe as a sieve?"

John chuckled. "Oh, I can easily put new hinges on it, Ginny. Get going, will you? And be sure to stop at Granny's and send Whiz right out here with the key to the padlock. Otherwise, after I've tacked the screen back, I'll be locked out."

"Oh, my goodness," Lucy cried, scrambling out of the window. "And I'd be locked in. The very thought gives me claustrophobia."

"Silly," Ginny snorted. "You and your ghosts and complexes. Come on. Keep an eye on the coffee, John. After the water has dripped down from the top, put the pot on the hot burner and turn it to 'simmer.' "

John glared at her. "Yes, ma'am, but don't forget I can't get back in until Whiz comes."

"Here he comes now," Lucy cried. "And Babs is not with him. I suppose she couldn't tear herself away from Riba's cake."

Whiz called out, "I forgot to give you the key. Sor-ree."

As Ginny biked toward him she said, "We didn't need it as you'll soon see."

John climbed through the Barn window then, and Whiz whistled shrilly. "Vandalism," he yelled. "Who committed the vandalism?"

Ginny and Lucy biked past him, leaving the explanation of the broken window to John. While they rode into town, Ginny brought Lucy up to date on all the recent events. Not until they stopped in front of the grocery store did she remember that she had forgotten to bring any money with her.

"This is really the end," she cried, dropping her bike on the sidewalk. "So much has happened since we opened that I've lost my mind."

"Never mind," Lucy said consolingly. "We can charge what we buy to Mother. She won't mind this once."

"I'll charge it to my own mother," Ginny said, "and give her the cash this evening. It was all my fault."

"No, it wasn't," Lucy said generously. "I should have thought of it, and so should John."

"But I'm the business manager," Ginny said as they walked into the store. "Although I wouldn't blame you all for firing me."

Lucy laughed. "Nobody else except John has any business sense." She hesitated. "Do you really think we ought to buy a whole dozen eggs? They might spoil before anyone eats them."

Ginny squared her shoulders resolutely. "We'll buy a whole dozen and a pound of sliced cheese and a pound of hamburger. A defeatist attitude isn't going to get us anywhere. Our classmates are going to run out of fifty-centses pretty soon. Then they'll have to stop going to the Inn until they get their next week's allowances."

"But," Lucy argued, "they won't have any money to spend at the Barn either. They may come out and play records and fool around, but that isn't going to get us anywhere either."

"I don't care," Ginny said, tossing her chestnut curls. "If it looks as though things are going to spoil, I'll sell the stuff to Mother. She's very understanding and co-operative about the whole thing."

"So is my mother," Lucy said. "Well, okay, let's stock up and not worry until we have to."

After they had filled both their bike baskets with supplies, they biked along Main Street to Orchard. Joe Dakor was standing in front of the Swap Shop and hailed them in a hoarse voice.

"Pardon my whisper," he said, grinning, "but my larynx is old and tired or something. What I want to know is, are you kids going to buy those heaters or not?"

Joe was a particular friend of Ginny's and she hastily decided to take advantage of that fact. "It's this way, Joe," she said, "we want them, but we can't buy them as long as that Lochinvar stays at the Inn."

Joe chuckled. "Kind of ruining your business, huh?"

"That's right," Ginny said, smiling sweetly. "But we have a feeling Hollywood will lure him away soon."

"I wouldn't be at all surprised," Joe said. "Not a-tall. I met him this morning, and he sure is a superman."

"Oh, did he come in the Swap Shop?" Ginny asked. "What for?"

"Just window shopping," Joe said. "He fell in love with the spinning wheel. It was nice of John to talk his grandmother into letting me keep it in the show window after you kids sold the business."

"John didn't have to talk his grandmother into letting you keep it, Joe," Ginny said. "Mrs. Blaketon was delighted to be able to do anything to help you make a success of the Shop. Everyone in town feels that way about it."

"I know," Joe said sheepishly. "They've all been swell to me, and to think I used to go around with a chip on my shoulder. I owe it all to you, Ginny," he went on. "That's why I feel like a heel crowding you about the heaters. But the trouble is that I could use some ready cash right now, and Doctor Bascom offered me a good price for them this morning."

"Oh, oh," Lucy moaned. "I was afraid of that. The cottage on the Blaketon place isn't insulated and there aren't any storm windows."

Ginny nodded forlornly. "And the Bascoms have a tiny baby. I imagine they want the heaters for the bathroom and the nursery."

"That's right," Joe said. "I'd do anything for you, Ginny, but Doc Bascom, well—he—when I was in trouble he stood up for me. And he's not what you'd call loaded with money. All he's got is the little practice Doc Hillman turned over to him."

"I know," Ginny said impulsively. "Dr. and Mrs. Bascom are simply darling. You sell them the heaters right away, Joe. We'll manage somehow." She knew that Joe felt as badly as she did and quickly changed the subject. "I wonder what made Lochinvar fall in love with the spinning wheel. He couldn't possibly know anything about antiques."

"Oh, but he does," Joe corrected her. "He put his finger unerringly on everything of real value in the show window."

"That's easily explained," Lucy said. "The original settlers of Kentucky brought some beautiful things with them from their homes in England, Scotland, and Ireland. The sight of that spinning wheel probably made Lochinvar homesick for the mountains."

Ginny laughed. "Everybody seems well informed on the Kentucky mountaineers except me. I thought you wore a dunce cap like mine, Lucy. Didn't you say you thought they lived on acorns or something?"

"I did," Lucy admitted, giggling. "But that's because I studied about them in the third grade, before we moved to Harristown. Things have changed since then."

"That's right," Joe agreed. "And if that hillbilly is the real McCoy, I'll eat the doormat."

"What makes you say that?" Ginny asked.

"His dialect," Joe said. "It's too, too pat. Oh, I don't blame him for living out his act. That's just good business. But, if he came from Kentucky, I'll bet it was from a big city like Louisville."

Suddenly Ginny remembered that the entertainer wore a pistol in a shoulder holster. "We've got to hurry," she said to Joe. "Come on, Lucy. John will have a fit if Officer Bill shows up before we do." As soon as they were out of Joe's hearing, she said, "Since you know so much about Kentucky, tell me about the feuds. In the books I read, the men were never without their shotguns, day and night."

"That's right," Lucy said. "And I guess they still carry them pretty much all the time. The mountaineers, I mean. They love to hunt, and sometimes a lucky shot at a rabbit might mean meat in the stew instead of just dumplings."

Ginny nodded. "Shotguns, not pistols. And this is a New York suburb. I doubt if Lochinvar will shoot the squirrels in the park."

Lucy giggled. "You *have* lost your mind, Ginny."

"No, I haven't," Ginny said soberly. "Lochinvar

carries a pistol in a shoulder holster, Lucy. I saw it when his shirt was drenched with water yesterday."

Lucy was so surprised she almost fell off her bike. "Oh, Ginny," she gasped. "You must have been mistaken. People like that don't carry guns. Why should they?"

"That's what I'd like to know," Ginny said. "The only explanation I can think of is that Lochinvar's family is feuding with another family. And maybe he followed one of the men north, seeking revenge."

"That's too dramatic an explanation," Lucy said firmly. "Your imagination is running away with you again." She thought for a minute. "A much more logical explanation is this. The pistol is only loaded with blank cartridges. It's just part of an act he does, maybe late at night, at closing time. I seem to remember that it's a custom of the mountaineers to shoot their guns in the air when a party is over."

"Aren't you smart?" Ginny asked admiringly. "I never would have thought of that. But now that you mention it, I remember Dad and Mother telling me when they came back from the New Orleans Mardi Gras that after the ball was over, the orchestra leader fired a pistol in the air and yelled, *'Le bal est fini!'* "

"Which brings us right back to our French homework," Lucy said, laughing. "Frankly, I can't wait for the Thanksgiving holidays, can you?"

They were passing the Reillys' home then, and

Mrs. Reilly called from the front porch. "Lucy, Ginny! Have you seen Babs?"

The girls got off their bikes and trundled them to the steps. "She's out at her grandmother's," Ginny said. "At least that's where she said she was going when she left school."

Mrs. Reilly shook her head worriedly. "She left there twenty minutes ago, and Riba says she didn't go in the direction of the Barn. She started back to town." Mrs. Reilly came down the steps, and shading her eyes from the bright afternoon sunlight with one hand, stared down the street. "I can't imagine what for, but Officer Bill is very anxious to get in touch with her."

Ginny caught her breath. Had Mr. Crayne heard about Babs's silly pranks, and, because the housekeeper had seen her sneaking down the Inn stairs after setting the booby trap, did he suspect Babs?

CHAPTER EIGHT

THE MISSING SANDWICHES

Ginny let out her breath in a long sigh. If Officer Bill wanted to see Babs, there could only be one answer. He wanted to question her about the booby trap. Lochinvar might not have reported the incident to the management, but the carpet in the hall outside his door had been soaked when the bucket fell.

She and John and the entertainer had mopped up a lot of the water, but the housekeeper's suspicions must have been aroused when she found so many damp towels in the rest room hamper and that section of the carpet soaking wet. And the janitor probably had reported that he left a bucket of water outside the White Elephant which was not there when he came back after being called away.

Upon hearing from both the housekeeper and the janitor, Mr. Crayne had undoubtedly questioned Lochinvar, who was occupying the White Elephant. Ginny was almost positive that the friendly singer would not have voluntarily done anything to get a youngster into trouble, but no one could blame him for not assuming the blame, especially since he had been the victim of the booby trap.

It looked as though Babs might well be involved in a scrape which might involve all the Hustlers and mean the end of the Snack Barn.

"Oh, thank goodness, here she comes now!" Mrs. Reilly's voice broke into Ginny's thoughts.

Ginny wheeled to face the park. Babs was strolling unconcernedly along, eating an ice-cream cone as though she hadn't a care in the world.

"Yoo-hoo, Babs," her mother called. "Officer Bill has been looking for you. Did he find you?"

Babs stopped short. She glanced nervously over first one shoulder and then the other. Her mother hurried across the street to meet her at the entrance to the park.

Lucy tugged at Ginny's arm. "Come on," she hissed. "Let her stew in her own juice. We've got to get this stuff out to the Barn before Officer—"

"Officer Bill," Ginny said sadly, "won't be there today. Look. He must have been trailing Babs and now he's caught up with her."

Sure enough, at that moment, the big burly policeman appeared on the path which was a short cut through the park. In two long strides he reached Babs's side and touched her shoulder. Babs jumped, and then stood as though she couldn't make up her mind what to do.

"We can't desert her now," Ginny said. "What she did, she did for the good of the Snack Barn, silly as both stunts were." As she spoke, she took the

Babs Seemed to Be in Trouble

packages from her bike basket and laid them on the Reillys' front steps. Lucy followed suit. Then they crossed the street.

"Now don't you worry, Mrs. Reilly," Officer Bill was saying in a soothing voice. "I just want to have a little talk with Babs."

"But what has she done, Bill?" Mrs. Reilly asked. "Oh, Babs, you didn't play hooky from school?"

Babs shook her head until her pigtails danced. Ginny could tell that she was very near to tears.

"Well, then," Mrs. Reilly said, starting back across the street, "I'll run along home. I imagine, Bill, you want to talk to the children about something connected with the Barn. I understand there are an endless number of rules you have to observe when you're dealing in food."

Officer Bill waited until Mrs. Reilly reached her front porch, then he said to Ginny, "This carrot-headed pal of yours stopped off at the Inn this morning on the way to school and let the air out of the tires on a jeep in the parking lot."

"Oh, Babs," Ginny cried. "You didn't."

Babs stared down at the scuffed toes of her moccasins.

"She did," Officer Bill said emphatically. "The parking-lot attendant saw a redheaded kid skulking around there at about eight-thirty."

"There are a lot of other redheaded girls in town," Lucy pointed out.

Officer Bill glared at her. "Yes, but none of them has a grudge against Lochinvar. None of them is connected with the Snack Barn. None of them would have any motive for causing the Inn's new entertainer trouble."

Ginny sank down on a park bench. "I simply can't believe it," she said. "We've told Babs at least a dozen times that she must not annoy that man. Oh, Babs, how *could* you?"

Babs blinked back tears. "He's ruined everything, that Lochinvar. And Whiz worked so hard. Every week-end and every minute after school fixing up the electrical equipment, and now—and now, we'll have to give up the Barn and we'll never have any more fun or excitement. Oh, oh," she sobbed. "Why doesn't he go away?"

Ginny glanced at Officer Bill. The expression on his big red face was one of sympathy, not anger. She sighed with relief. He would give Babs another chance before reporting her to her parents. "I'm awfully sorry this happened, Officer Bill," Ginny said quickly. "And I'm sure Babs won't be silly any more. She'll go and apologize to Lochinvar right away, won't you, Babs?"

Babs stubbornly set her jaw. "I'm not sorry. I wish I'd stuck nails in the tires of his old jeep."

Ginny could cheerfully have slapped Babs at that moment. Instead of being grateful that news of her other pranks hadn't yet reached the ears of Officer

Bill, she was behaving in a manner which was sure to get all the Hustlers in trouble.

Ginny mentally counted to ten. Then she got up and took Babs's hand. "We'll go with you," she said. "Lucy and I. That'll make it easier. But you must apologize to Lochinvar immediately. And first you must thank Officer Bill for not reporting you to your mother when she was right here a minute ago."

Then it dawned on Babs for the first time what a narrow escape she had had. Instantly she was contrite. "I'm sorry," she said humbly, smiling through her tears at the policeman. "You're a very good sport, Officer Bill, and I promise I won't do anything silly any more."

"See that you don't," he advised, striding away. "I'm too busy these days to keep an eye on a mischievous leprechaun like you." He stopped before crossing the street and added over one broad shoulder: "That Lochinvar is the best friend you ever had. Said if it was a kid who let the air out of his tires I was to skip it. Said his favorite pastime when he was a kid was letting air out of folks' tires." He ended in a loud chuckle and Ginny knew that Babs was forgiven as far as the policeman was concerned.

"You don't have to go to the Inn with me," Babs said, all smiles now. "If Lochinvar let air out of people's tires when he was a kid, he won't be very mad. And," she added, "I am really sorry now. I thought he'd tattled to Officer Bill, but I guess it was the parking-lot attendant."

"All right," Ginny said. "Go along, and be as sweet and humble as possible. Come on, Lucy." Half way across the street she stopped and called back to Babs, "How did you know the jeep belonged to him anyway?"

"Because," Babs said smugly, "I saw him drive past the house in it yesterday morning. It was just getting light and I happened to wake up early on Sunday for once, and looked out the window and by he went in a jeep. It was the only one in the parking lot."

"Fate," Ginny said to Lucy as she reloaded her bike basket, "plays right into the hands of redheaded people. It's hard for me to believe that Babs was out of bed at dawn yesterday, especially since she was allowed to stay up past her bedtime Saturday night."

"And how about Lochinvar?" Lucy asked. "You would think he would have slept late, too. The Inn doesn't close until one in the morning and he must have been singing until the bitter end."

They started off for the Barn and Ginny said, "He's not supposed to sing after the Inn stops serving dinners, but Saturday night he created such a riot he did keep on until the bitter end. Almost everyone who was at the Inn that night slept much later than they usually do. My parents did. I can't imagine why Lochinvar was up and around at the crack of dawn."

"I can't either," Lucy said. "But I guess it isn't any of our business."

"I guess it isn't," Ginny agreed. "But I was just thinking about that pistol. If it's part of an act he does when the Inn closes, why was he wearing it yesterday afternoon? I should think the holster would bother him when he plays the accordion."

"I don't think anything like that would bother him," Lucy said.

"You can say that again," Ginny said, "after you've seen him."

"I have seen him," Lucy said.

"When?" Ginny demanded. "Don't tell me you were up at dawn yesterday, too."

"No," Lucy said, "but I *was* up at dawn today. Last night I got to worrying about those French verbs and decided to set my alarm for six instead of seven. I was yawning out of my window which faces the park, trying to wake up, when I saw him walking briskly along the path."

"How did you know it was Lochinvar?" Ginny asked. "Was he wearing his costume—the red-checked shirt and dungarees?"

Lucy nodded. "And, don't forget, I'd seen his picture in the paper. Besides there isn't anybody else in town except Officer Bill who is as tall as that with shoulders as broad. And *he* would have been in uniform."

Ginny giggled. "Outside of their builds, they

wouldn't be mistaken for each other, even if they wore the same clothes. Officer Bill has a nice cheery face, but he isn't exactly handsome." She thought for a minute. "Lochinvar must be one of those super people who don't need much sleep. Do you suppose he keeps in such good physical condition by taking long walks at dawn?"

"It baffles me what he does at that time of the morning," Lucy said. "Nobody else in this town except the police wander around before it gets light."

"That's perfectly true," Ginny agreed. "He's getting to be a mystery man, he and his shoulder holster. Do you think Joe was right when he hinted that Lochinvar only *talks* like a Kentucky mountaineer?"

"Joe's awfully smart," Lucy said thoughtfully. "But I wouldn't know."

"I wouldn't either," Ginny admitted. "But I loved the way he talked. He kept dropping his g's and prefixing a's so that the words sort of flowed together in a singsongy way. But it could be all part of his act as Joe said."

She thought about it all for several minutes and then said, "That business about his letting air out of people's tires when he was a kid. That sounds as though he grew up in a city or town, not a mountain village. If hillbillies were so poor a few years ago that they ate practically nothing but acorns, I can't believe his neighbors had trucks and cars."

"That's right," Lucy said. "They mostly rode on mules and plowed with them, too. I can distinctly remember the pictures in my third grade book."

Ginny sighed. "It's all too, too baffling. But it is beginning to sound as though my feud theory isn't so fantastic. If he's on the trail of somebody, he'd almost have to search for clues in the early morning. That's about the only time he wouldn't attract attention."

"That's the one time he'd attract the attention of the police," Lucy pointed out tiredly. "Let's not talk about it any more. Sometimes, Ginny, your detective mind gets boring."

Ginny laughed. "I'm sorry. I must be particularly boring to a well-informed person like you right now. All I really know about mountaineers is that they were always 'a-feudin' and a-fightin'.' "

When they reached the Barn, the boys had already repaired the screen and were puttying in the new pane of glass.

"Took you long enough," Whiz said sarcastically. "The coffee cooked away to the last drop while you were gone."

"We were delayed by your twin," Lucy informed him. "If it hadn't been for Ginny's quick tact, Babs would be in jail, or anyway, in the doghouse at home."

"Gleeps!" Whiz yelled. "I was afraid her crimes would catch up with her. John and I were just talking about the booby trap. Honestly, I've a good mind to go home and drown that dimwit in the washtub. She deserves it."

"Calm down," Ginny said. "All is well. She is at the Inn now humbly apologizing to Lochinvar. And, Whiz Reilly," she went on sternly, "you're not so hot yourself. The idea of your eating up all those leftover sandwiches which I carefully put in the refrigerator for snacks today."

Whiz dropped his putty knife. "*I* ate the sandwiches?" he demanded hotly. "Listen, Ginny Gordon, just because you're a year older than I am and have solved a couple of mysteries, doesn't mean you can go around accusing me of crimes I didn't commit." He picked up the putty knife and shook it under her nose. "I never even opened the door of the refrigerator when I came out last evening!"

Ginny stared at him, her brown eyes wide with amazement. "But, Whiz," she asked in a mollified tone of voice, "who else could have taken them? I'm sorry I accused you, but I just took it for granted that you must have eaten them."

All three of them followed Ginny as she hurried to open the refrigerator door. Way back on one of the shelves was an almost empty jar of relish. Ginny yanked it out and set it on the counter.

"See for yourselves," she said. "The refrigerator is absolutely empty!"

CHAPTER NINE

"WE'VE BEEN ROBBED!"

"But it couldn't have been Henderson," Ginny said for the fourth time. "Why would he swipe some sandwiches and leave five dollars in the cash box?"

"All right, have it your own way," Whiz said impatiently. "I still think Henderson is a dimwit like Babs. He saw you put the sandwiches in the refrigerator and later, because he was hungry, he couldn't resist the temptation to eat them while he was ripping the hinges off the cash box."

"You said he was fat," Lucy reminded Ginny. "People like that are always hungry. And Dr. Bascom told me the other day that older people, unless there's something wrong with them, just don't get fat unless they eat between meals."

"Let's not get sidetracked by a dietary discussion," John said as he finished putting new hinges on the cash box. "If you'd all listen a minute, I'd like to present my own theory."

"Go right ahead," Whiz said. "I'm almost as hoarse as Joe Dakor from arguing with Ginny."

"Henderson is hoarse too," Ginny said thoughtfully. "I wonder why."

John sighed. "Sometimes, Ginny, that inquiring

mind of yours gets me down. Can't you stick to one subject for the next three minutes?"

"For goodness sake," Ginny said crossly. "I'm getting sick of being picked on by you people. On the way out here, Lucy accused me of being boring. Then Whiz snapped at me, armed with a putty knife, and now you, John—"

Everyone laughed, and Ginny couldn't help joining in. "I'm sorry, Mr. President," she said, bowing to John. "You have the floor. I promise not to interrupt even if Mr. Chadwell appears and demands his money at the point of a gun."

"There she goes off on another tangent," Whiz said, his green eyes twinkling. "You've got a mind that leaps around like a mountain goat."

"Speaking of mountains," Ginny said to him, "do you think that Kentucky mountaineers have lots of cars, Whiz?"

John threw up his hands in mock anguish. "I give up. I may as well go home and type out my theory and then ask Ginny's father to have it mimeographed. That's the only way the rest of you will ever know what I think about the mystery of the stolen sandwiches."

Ginny promptly sat down and covered her mouth with both hands. She rapidly blinked her eyes at John to let him know that she was silenced for an indefinite period.

John, half-smiling and half-serious, sat down opposite her. "My almost forgotten theory is this. After Henderson broke into the Barn and departed with the envelope, a tramp came along. Seeing the open window, he climbed in and spent the night here. When he awoke in the morning he naturally peeked into the refrigerator. What tramp could resist those neatly wrapped sandwiches to sustain him while he traveled north on the highway?"

"That," Whiz said decisively, "makes a lot of sense. Ungag yourself, Ginny. Speak, mastermind." He snapped his fingers at her.

"Bow wow," Ginny barked obligingly. "First I'm boring, then I accuse innocent people; after that I'm a mountain goat, and now I'm a talking dog." She shrugged her slim shoulders. "I think I'll get a job at the Inn. Even Lochinvar couldn't compete with anyone as versatile as I seem to be."

"Oh, Ginny," Lucy cried contritely. "We really hurt your feelings. I'm *so* sorry. You never really bore me. It's just that I don't think we should waste time worrying about what Lochinvar did in his childhood."

"Definitely, no," Ginny said. "And John's theory is obviously the answer to the mystery of the missing sandwiches." She got up and slipped into her short tweed jacket. "Now that you've repaired the window and the cash box, we have nothing to worry about, so I'm going home. The rest of you can lock up."

"Wait a minute, Ginny," John said gently. "I

know how disappointed you are in the Snack Barn.
Since it was your idea, I guess it meant more to you
than the rest of us. But you were in an optimistic
mood when you and Lucy biked into town for supplies. What happened to depress you?"

Ginny came back and sat down again. "The heaters, John," she said. "You tell him, Lucy. I can't
bear to talk about it."

Lucy quickly explained.

"If it had been anybody else but those darling
Bascoms," Ginny said, "and if the weather maps
didn't show that there's a cold front moving toward
us from the northwest, and the sandwiches gone, and
the window and screen and cash box broken, and
nobody, not even Officer Bill here to eat what Lucy
and I bought today." She covered her face with her
hands. "I made up my mind not to get discouraged,
but—but I give up."

Lucy impulsively threw her arms around her best
friend. "Don't cry, Ginny. Please don't. It'll work
out somehow. Lochinvar will leave town soon. Wait
and see." She snatched her jacket off a bench and
ran out.

"Now, I've made *her* cry," Ginny said with a rue-
ful grin.

"I feel like crying myself," Whiz said sympathetically. "Even if we could arouse the town fathers
into tarring and feathering Lochinvar and running
him out of town on a rail, it wouldn't do us any good

now. Brand new electric heaters will cost more than we've got in the bank."

John nodded worriedly. "Not to mention what they'll do to our meter every time we plug them in." He strode over to the window. "Holy cow," he muttered. "Here comes Babs pedaling as though the devil were after her. What kind of a scrape do you suppose she's in now?"

Babs burst into the Barn, her pigtails flapping around her face. "News," she cried. "Good news! I'm sure he'll be fired. What a break."

"Calm down, Paul Revere," Whiz said. "Who is going to fire whom? And why?"

"Lochinvar," she yelled. "He didn't show up for tea, and Mr. Crayne was wild. The place was packed and jammed and the high-school kids whistled and stamped until he ordered them all to leave. It was then that he explained that Lochinvar must have been unavoidably detained someplace, and he sounded awfully cross."

Ginny sighed. "I wouldn't blame Lochinvar for quitting after what you've been doing to him practically ever since he arrived."

"Oh, he didn't quit," Babs assured her. "The jeep is still in the parking lot behind the Inn. I made sure of that before I bothered to write him, you know."

"You wrote him?" Whiz bellowed. "What on earth for?"

"Stop screaming at me," Babs screamed.

Whiz stuck his fingers in his ears. "Deafened," he groaned. "Stone deaf at the age of thirteen. And all due to my own twin sister."

"Stop it," John commanded. "Why did you write Lochinvar, Babs?"

"Because," she told him more quietly, "Ginny told me I had to apologize immediately. And since he wasn't there I simply sat down at the desk in the lobby and wrote him a note which I gave to the front desk clerk who put it in Lochinvar's box."

Ginny frowned. "What did you say in the note, Babs?"

"Just this," Babs said airily. " 'I think you're simply wonderful, Mr. Lochinvar, and I won't even come near the Inn again. Love, Babs.' Cute, huh?"

"Oh, fine," Whiz groaned. "Cute as a snake bite. Can't you see, lamebrain, that it doesn't make any sense?"

"Don't you realize, Babs," Ginny asked patiently, "that the man doesn't even know your name? Officer Bill is awfully careful about things like that. He wasn't absolutely sure that it was you the parking-lot attendant saw this morning until you confessed."

"I never thought of that," Babs admitted. "I'd better write him another note explaining the first one. I could say, 'Dear Mr. Lochinvar, I'm sorry the first note doesn't make sense, but I'll never do it again.' "

"Do," Whiz said with a snort of disgust. "And sign it 'Betty Grable.' Then he can have you arrested for forgery and all of our troubles will be over."

John was shaking with laughter. "I think she had better let well enough alone. One baffling note from Babs is about all the man could stand and keep his sanity."

"I think so too," Ginny agreed. "Next time one of us is out there we can explain everything."

"Then you don't think Mr. Crayne will fire him?" Babs asked forlornly.

"Of course not," Whiz said. "Managers, *smart* managers, don't fire entertainers like that simply because they were unavoidably detained someplace."

"I wonder what detained him and where?" Ginny asked. "Since his jeep is there, he couldn't be far from town if he left it at all. What I mean is, a blowout or engine trouble couldn't have detained him."

"I can't waste my sympathy on him," Whiz said. "If ever a man looks as though he could take care of himself, Lochinvar is that man."

It was on the tip of Ginny's tongue to tell the others that the hillbilly singer carried a gun, but she quickly decided against it. She had had enough teasing for one day. John and Whiz would be sure to say that she was only letting her imagination run away with her. And as for Babs—Ginny shuddered to think of the garbled version that would spread through school the next day. Why, it would be just like Babs to end up saying that she knew for a fact that Lochinvar was an armed escaped convict!

In study period next day in school, Ginny could not make herself start the composition her English teacher had assigned. Her thoughts kept wandering to Lochinvar. Why did he carry a gun? What did he do early in the mornings? What had unavoidably detained him? Why hadn't he telephoned Mr. Crayne that he would be detained?

When the last bell rang the only word she had written in her notebook was "hillbilly." And that gave Ginny an idea. She would write a composition on Kentucky mountaineers. Whiz, in exchange for coaching in math, would give her all the facts she needed.

When she met him on the front steps of the school and suggested the idea to him, he heartily agreed.

"You could, of course," he told her, "get all the dope from clips in the morgue at the *News*. But that would be taking advantage of us kids whose dads aren't newspapermen."

"There wouldn't be anything but brief, cold facts in the *News* files," Ginny said. "I want some colorful material. For instance, do the people still use mules or do they have tractors and trucks and jeeps?"

"All four nowadays," Whiz said. "There were some swell pictures in a magazine I read recently. I'll find it for you."

At the bike stand they met the other Hustlers and they all rode straight out to the Barn.

"We'd better not waste any time today," Ginny said as John turned his key in the padlock. "Officer Bill, and maybe Mike, will be sure to show up for a snack. They promised, you know, to come out whenever they could."

John was staring at the padlock. "Look at the scratches on this thing," he said. "They weren't there when we bought it. It was brand new."

"Henderson," Ginny said. "First he tried to pick the lock with his knife or nail file, then when he couldn't, he broke in through the window."

"I don't remember seeing the scratches yesterday," John said. "Do you, Whiz?"

"I didn't really look at it," Whiz said. "We were in such a hurry to get in and putty the window pane in place, I didn't notice anything. I don't even remember locking or unlocking the door. Did I or did you?"

"You unlocked it," John said. "You had my key, remember?"

"You locked up when we left yesterday afternoon," Ginny told John. "But it was getting dark so I don't think you could have seen any scratches." She led the way inside. "What difference does it make? Henderson must have made them."

Babs listlessly ducked under the counter and opened the cupboard. She picked up a can and her eyes brightened. "Oh, let's open some tuna fish. I adore tuna fish sandwiches."

"All right," Ginny said, taking a stick of butter out of the refrigerator. "The can opener is hanging on the back of the cupboard door."

"No, it isn't," Babs said. "Two spatulas, a long fork, a long spoon, but no can opener."

"That's just like you, Babs," Lucy cried impatiently. "The can opener *has* to be on its hook. I remember distinctly yesterday when I was putting away the things Ginny and I bought in town that it was there. That sharp pointed thing that slides up and down snagged a hole in my sweater sleeve."

Babs giggled. "Maybe it's still clinging to your sweater."

"Don't be silly, Babs," Ginny said sharply. "Look for it. Maybe one of us knocked it on the floor and it got kicked under the counter."

Dutifully, Babs got down on her hands and knees and crawled up and down under the counter. "Nothing but a little dust," she reported. "And don't tell me that it's my turn to sweep. The floor isn't that dirty."

"Help her look for it, please, boys," Ginny said. "We can't pry the tops off the jars without it."

"I can pry them off with my knife," John said. "And let's have some of that pineapple and cream cheese mixture. You wouldn't believe it, but Mike is very fond of it."

"That's good," Ginny said. "We have one jar which we didn't use on the opening day."

"I'll get it," Babs offered. "Is it in the cupboard or on one of the shelves by the sink?"

"In the cupboard," Ginny told her. "Lucy and I decided in the beginning to keep anything that might be knocked off and get broken in the cupboard. All the jars are in there."

"Yummy-yum," Babs mumbled. "Pimento and olive. Cream cheese and deviled ham. Nothing with pineapple, Ginny."

"That," Lucy said, "I happen to know is there. I moved it back to make room for the mayonnaise yesterday afternoon."

"But it isn't," Babs said. "I've looked twice. There's nothing but air behind the mayonnaise."

"Nothing but air?" Lucy gasped. "Why, I pushed several little things back to make room for that big jar. Ginny insisted on buying a quart because it's cheaper that way."

"Let me look," Ginny said. "Why, the peanut butter is gone too. There wasn't much left, but enough for a couple of sandwiches. I made a mental note of it yesterday so we'd be sure to buy some more if we used it up today."

Lucy promptly joined her in front of the cupboard. "Why, Ginny," she said after a quick glance inside. "That tiny can of shrimp is gone, too. Who could have taken those things?"

"Several Jars Have Disappeared!"

Ginny reached up to the shelf by the sink and opened the bread box. "Just as I thought," she said, "a loaf of bread has disappeared. We bought two loaves and now there's only one." Through the window above the sink she could see Officer Bill trudging down the lane. "Never mind," she said hastily to Lucy. "We have plenty of stuff for cheeseburgers. Officer Bill, thank heavens, is crazy about them."

"But, Ginny," Lucy whispered, "aren't you going to tell Officer Bill that we've been robbed?"

"No, I'm not," Ginny said firmly. "After Babs's little scene with him yesterday, the less we say to Officer Bill, the better. Besides, there may be some simple explanation of what happened to our missing supplies."

"But John will tell him," Lucy argued under her breath. "He's super sensible about things like that."

"John," Ginny whispered back, "is also super loyal. He won't breathe a word until after consulting the rest of us."

"I hope you're right," Lucy said doubtfully. "If your mother finds out you're involved in another mystery, not to mention the fact that a thief—" She stopped, for Officer Bill was coming in the door.

Whiz, who had been searching for the can opener under one of the tables, scrambled to his feet. "Hi, Officer Bill," he greeted the big policeman. "You're just in time, and I hope you brought a finger-printing outfit with you. We've been robbed!"

CHAPTER TEN

BREAD AND GLUE

Ginny's one impulse was to vault over the counter and clap her hand across Whiz's mouth. Why did he have to blurt out to Officer Bill that they had been robbed? She could almost see the write-up in the *News* and the expression on her father's face as he said, "As far as you're concerned, Ginny, the Snack Barn is out of bounds until the thief has been captured."

For one awful minute Officer Bill stood in the doorway, practically gaping at Whiz. Then Ginny came to her senses. "We certainly have been robbed, Officer Bill," she said, forcing a wide smile to her stiff lips. "And I hope you take the matter up with the Chief of Police. Somebody swiped our ten-cent can opener."

The tall policeman guffawed and moved across the room to lean his elbows on the counter, grinning at Ginny. "A ten-cent can opener, eh? Well, well, well. Whom do you suspect?"

"Mike, frankly," Ginny said, grinning back at him. "I think he figured that if we didn't have a can opener we'd have to serve fresh cream instead of evaporated milk."

Whiz, very red in the face, gesticulated wildly behind the officer's back to show that he had caught on. John's face was expressionless as he occupied himself with prying the lid off a jar with his knife. Babs looked bewildered, but out of the corner of one eye, Ginny saw Lucy move down to the cupboard with her finger on her lips.

"Mike, huh?" Officer Bill was saying. "So Suspect Number One is the janitor of the Canton Building?"

"And Lochinvar," Lucy said, obviously trying to be helpful by keeping the matter under the heading of a joke. "He's Suspect Number Two. I don't imagine they have new-fangled inventions like can openers where he comes from. I really think," she said, pretending to be very serious, "that you ought to arrest him at once."

Officer Bill, completely overcome with laughter, staggered backward and collapsed heavily in a chair.

"What's so funny about that?" Babs demanded before anyone could stop her. "He *is* a suspicious character, if you ask me. Oh, I know he was a good sport not to tattle on me, but why is he up and around so early in the morning? I saw him at dawn Sunday, and Lucy—"

"And you?" Officer Bill interrupted, sobering immediately. "Why were you up and around so early in the morning, may I ask?" He glared at Babs and Lucy.

Babs tossed her pigtails, but Lucy hastened to

reply before matters got worse. "We were both home in our own rooms, Officer Bill, when we saw him. And we were just joking when we said he was a suspicious character."

"That's right," John said, coming to the rescue. "And the joke is old and tired now. How about you girls rustling up some food for Officer Bill?"

"Cheeseburger or a Western sandwich?" Ginny asked, tying on her apron.

"That reminds me," Officer Bill said. "I brought you kids a pot of chives. The Missus said you'd have trouble keeping onions from sprouting in this weather, but chives, she said, if you keep 'em from going to seed, go on forever. Left the pot outside the door."

"That was awfully thoughtful of your wife, Officer Bill," Ginny said gratefully. "Chives are even more delicious in a Western than onions."

Officer Bill nodded. "Cream cheese and chives are tasty, too," he said. "But that Mike, he won't touch cream cheese unless it's loaded with pineapple."

"We had some of that spread," Babs blurted. "But it mysteriously disappeared, too, like the can opener."

Ginny sucked in her breath. Why *did* Babs have to keep on saying and doing things that would eventually get them all into trouble? She glanced at Officer Bill and saw with relief that he was smiling.

"Then Mike's your man," he said to Babs. "Even

a rookie cop would suspect him if both a can opener and a jar of his favorite mix are missing." He turned around to Whiz. "You've got an amateur finger-printing outfit," he said. "Why don't you get to work? Are you boys going to let Ginny solve all the mysteries around here?" He chuckled loudly.

Whiz grinned weakly. "I'm fresh out of iodine crystals. We'd better call in the FBI, Officer Bill."

"Speaking of which," the policeman said, "what are you kids going to do about heating this place when this unseasonal weather comes to an end? Indian summer won't last too long."

"Oh, goodness," Ginny said, setting a sizzling cheeseburger on the table in front of him. "Are there Federal laws which govern the temperature of public eating places?"

Officer Bill laughed. "I'm thinking of the laws which govern human nature. This place will be as cold as a barn soon." He roared with laughter at his own joke.

When he subsided, Ginny told him about the electric heaters they had planned to buy.

Officer Bill frowned sympathetically. "You kids have had a lot of tough breaks, but don't give up. What you really ought to have out here, anyway, is a little oil burner with an electric thermostat. Otherwise, when you unplug the heaters and go home, the pipes may freeze during the night."

Whiz whistled. "Gleeps," he groaned. "None of

us, not even I, thought of that."

"I thought of it," John admitted, "but I didn't say anything because there isn't anything we can do about it until we make some money. Even *little* automatic oil burners are expensive."

"Well, now," the friendly policeman said, spooning sugar into his coffee, "I'll let you in on a secret. I wasn't supposed to say anything about it until we saw how this Snack Barn worked out. But a lot of the boys at the Station House who have kids your age have wanted a PAL for a long time. When you started this project they said, 'If it's a success, that'll be our spearhead.' "

"I don't follow you," Ginny said. "PAL headquarters are always located at the local police station, aren't they?"

"They are," Officer Bill said. "But there's no reason why your Barn couldn't be our official snack bar and recreation center." He turned to John. "A lot of the boys are wondering if your grandmother might sell us the field that lies between here and her house. It would be a grand place for baseball, basketball, hockey, and track. In winter we could flood it and freeze it for ice skating."

"Granny," John said without a moment's hesitation, "would donate the field to PAL if Harristown had one."

"I thought so," Officer Bill said. "And a lot of other people would donate money for sports equipment. The salaries for athletic instructors would also be raised by public subscription."

The five Hustlers grouped themselves around him, listening attentively. "That was more or less our own idea," Ginny said. "We thought the Barn might develop into a community project if it was run under adult supervision. I hoped it might eventually become the Harristown Youth Center. You know, a place where an underprivileged boy like Joe Dakor was after his father died, could come and have fun."

"That's right," John added. "There are a lot of boys and girls in town who, like Joe, had tough breaks." He smiled soberly. "Tough breaks which have made them a little tough."

Officer Bill nodded understandingly. "We don't have any wayward minors in town," he said, "but call it what you will, we need a Youth Center. The school facilities don't cover enough of the time when school isn't in session." He cleared his throat. "And now, with the teen-agers stamping and whistling at the Inn afternoons and week-ends, I think we'd better get organized. The Inn is no place for youngsters. It's run strictly for adults, and a fine place it is, with an excellent reputation, but still, no place for youngsters."

"It's all that Lochinvar's fault," Lucy put in. "If it hadn't been for him, our Barn would have been such a success it could have become the spearhead you were talking about."

"It's really too bad," Ginny added. "Because you see, Officer Bill, we didn't plan to make a profit on the Barn. We figured that if and when it became a community project we would have recovered our original investment. We were going to have a lending library, you know, books and magazines, and John was making a Ping-pong table. But now—"

The officer cleared his throat again. "Now, don't get discouraged," he said, looking very uncomfortable. "Just hang on for a while longer. Something may happen which may mean you can buy an oil burner yet." He put a fifty-cent piece down by his plate and left without waiting for his change.

Ginny stared at John. "Why, he looked so guilty you'd almost think he was Lochinvar's manager!"

"He certainly did," John agreed. "I don't get it. He's trying to tell us something, but it's over my head."

"Mine, too," Whiz said. "Methinks Officer Bill is getting devious in his old age. He used to be as blunt as Babs, and almost as tactless."

"I don't know what you're fussing about," Lucy said impatiently. "It's all as plain as plain can be. The police force isn't any more crazy about Lochinvar than we are. I wouldn't be at all surprised if they picked him up on a vagrancy charge yet and made him leave town."

Whiz hooted. "A little knowledge of the law is

more dangerous than none at all. Hasn't your un-spongelike mind, Lucy, absorbed any other law except the one about vagrants?"

Lucy flushed. "I know a lot about traffic regula-tions and parking rules, but that law about tramps seems so handy. I can't seem to get it out of my head. Lochinvar entertains all week, but he only gets a salary for entertaining week-ends. Why doesn't that make him a vagrant from Monday through Friday?"

"Because," John explained patiently, "he gets his room and meals instead of a salary."

"That's rather odd in itself," Ginny said thought-fully. "His meals couldn't cost Mr. Crayne much since he buys everything in large quantities at whole-sale prices. And as for the White Elephant, it wouldn't be occupied at this time of the year any-way. It's a horrid little hole-in-the-wall, and Loch-invar obviously isn't getting proper maid service, otherwise someone would have found the accordion under his bed long before he did."

"The question you're leading up to," John put in, "is why such a talented performer should work for so little?"

Ginny nodded. "And the answer must be that he's an honest-to-goodness hillbilly with very simple tastes."

"I still think he's a vagrant," Lucy said stub-bornly.

"Speaking of which," Whiz said, "who stole our

can opener?"

"And the stuff in the cupboard?" Lucy added.

"And the loaf of bread?" Ginny finished. "A tramp, of course."

"How smart of you, Ginny," Babs said. "He picked the lock with the can opener."

Whiz hid his face in the crook of his arm. "Take her away," he howled. "Out of my sight, moron."

"What did I say wrong now?" Babs asked plaintively.

Ginny laughed and explained. "The can opener was *inside*, Babs, when we locked up yesterday." She turned to Whiz, frowning. "Stop clowning, will you? Nothing of any real value was stolen, but don't you think you ought to pull yourself together and buy a padlock that can't be picked?"

"There is no such thing," Whiz retorted. "Almost any lock can be picked by the right person."

"What do you mean by the right person?" Ginny asked.

"A burglar," Whiz said. "Or a detective." He grinned at Lucy. "Or one of your ghosts. Although I suppose your invisible friends laugh at locksmiths."

Lucy's cheeks flamed with anger. "A lot of people more intelligent than you, Whiz Reilly," she told him defensively, "believe in the supernatural."

"Name one," Whiz said.

"A. Conan Doyle," Ginny said promptly. "Will

you please stop clowning, Whiz? If we can't keep tramps out of here, what are we going to do?"

"We should, of course," John said slowly, "report the thefts to the police. And I was all for that idea until Officer Bill began talking about putting the official PAL stamp of approval on the Barn."

"That's right," Ginny said quickly. "When the other officers come out here, we don't want them to come with their fingerprinting equipment. We want them to come and oh and ah over what we've done to the old barn."

"At the rate we're going," Whiz said sourly, "they'll 'come to bury Caesar, not to praise him.'"

"A little knowledge of Shakespeare," Lucy jeered, "is more dangerous than none."

"I can quote from Scott, too," Whiz said airily. " 'So faithful in love, so dauntless in war, There never was knight like the young Lochinvar.'"

"Let's get back to locksmiths," John said.

"I thought you said tramps didn't break into locked places," Ginny said.

"How did we know an ex-burglar tramp was going to happen along?" Whiz demanded. "The point is that he's been and gone. The chances of the padlock getting picked again are practically nil."

"I think you've got something there, Whiz," John said. "Almost any tramp will climb in through the broken window of a barn, but it's rare that one will pick a lock. I don't think we'll have any more trouble, Ginny."

"I see," she said thoughtfully. "The two thefts were just a coincidence. I wonder why the lock-picker didn't break into the cash box while he was about it. I didn't think ex-burglars had any scruples."

"Oh, oh," Lucy cried. "Maybe he did. Have you looked, Ginny?"

Ginny nodded. "I didn't have time to count the change, of course, but it looked like it was all there. Frankly," she went on, "I'm going to take it home with me every night from now on." She got up and went behind the counter to dump the contents of the cash box in an empty cracker can.

"Are you going to lug that heavy thing to school every day?" Lucy asked.

Ginny laughed. "No, I'll stop at home for it on the way out here. It'll only take a minute."

"Why did you dump it out of the cash box?" Whiz asked. "It's got a handle and is easier to carry than that cracker can."

"Because," Ginny said, 'I keep petty cash vouchers and our bank pass book in the bottom section. There's no sense in toting those back and forth every day. Nobody is going to steal them. I'm not going to bother to lock the box after this."

Whiz turned exasperatedly to John. "After all the time and money you spent putting on new hinges!"

"Oh, well," John said easily, "the time may come when Ginny will decide again to leave money in the box overnight. I frankly think it's perfectly safe."

"What we ought to do," Ginny said suddenly, "instead of sitting around here moaning and groaning, is to think up a cute ad which Dad will run in the *News*. He won't charge us much for the space."

"What kind of an ad?" Lucy asked. "Everybody in this part of Westchester must have seen the opening day notice which appeared on Friday and Saturday."

Ginny went out to her bike basket and came back with a pad and some pencils. "There's still a chance we might be able to rent the Barn to people planning private parties. With the Inn so packed and jammed at teatime now, this is really the only place where people can give little receptions."

"What a wonderful idea," Lucy cried.

"You're a smart gal, Ginny," John said admiringly. "And I know of someone we might interest."

"Who?" Ginny asked excitedly.

"Betty Leland," John told her. "Carson was telling me the other day that they plan to get married very soon. Mrs. Arnold is going to pay for all their wedding expenses. And this would be an ideal place for the reception."

"You're perfectly right," Ginny said. "The Arnold mansion is way, way out at the other end of town. Besides," she went on, "Mrs. Arnold's big parlor is so cluttered up with massive antiques you couldn't get many people in it."

"Don't build your hopes up too high," John said cautiously. "Betty's parents may want to have the reception at their home."

"I doubt it," Ginny said. "Their apartment is absolutely tiny, John, and both Betty and Carson have loads of friends."

"We don't have to soak them much for the use of the Barn," Whiz put in. "But we can charge like anything for cakes and canapes. The Inn does."

"I know Riba will make dozens of her cute little cupcakes and star-shaped cookies for us," Babs said. "I wish I had some right now."

"Mother will give me her canape recipes, I know," Lucy said, "and show us how to make them look attractive."

"My mother will help, too," Ginny said. "She's famous for divine appetizers she whips up out of avocados, cheese and lots of other stuff. She serves it with potato chips."

"Stop!" Babs wailed. "I could eat wood shavings at the moment."

"That reminds me," John interrupted. "I left a good piece of pine board in front of the Barn on Saturday, and I haven't seen it since. Did any of you move it?"

"How big was it, John?" Ginny asked. "I don't remember seeing it."

"About the length and width of the wall benches," he told her. "I planned to build outdoor benches on both sides of the door in front, you know, but I ran out of materials."

"I remember seeing it when I went home Saturday evening," Lucy said. "I thought how ugly it looked and wondered why you hadn't put it in back where it wouldn't be seen."

"I would have put it in back," John said, "but I was afraid the trash collectors might take it by mistake."

"I guess they picked it up anyway," Whiz said. "They're always snatching up my most valued possessions which they refer to as junk."

"They don't come on Sundays," John said. "It was there Saturday night, and it was not there Sunday morning."

"A tramp tramped off with it," Ginny said with a giggle. "Lucy's vagrants are getting to be nuisances."

"A tramp," John said soberly, "wouldn't have any use for a heavy piece of board like that. And another thing that baffles me is that the same person who swiped the sandwiches Sunday night, must have gone off with my glue."

Babs laughed. "Why, he must have been as starving as I am. Although I draw the line at glue."

"Wood shavings, yes," Whiz said, "but glue, no. What a birdlike appetite, my little woodpecker."

"There is a connection," John said soberly. "A piece of wood and a pot of glue."

"Oh, my goodness," Ginny said wearily. "Tramps

are not only ex-burglars, it seems, they're carpenters, too. How do you know the glue is missing, John?"

"Because," he told her, "when I looked in the tool chest for hammer and tacks Monday afternoon it wasn't there. And it was there Saturday morning."

"Squirrels," Babs said suddenly. "Riba says the ones in Granny's attic are regular magpies."

Whiz tapped his forehead with his forefinger. "When squirrels start building their nests out of pine board and glue, then I'll know I'm nuts."

"If peculiar things don't stop happening around here," Ginny said, pushing back her chair, "we'll all go crazy. I'm going home and get Dad to help me write that ad."

CHAPTER ELEVEN

Ginny put her bike in the garage and, with her schoolbooks under her arm, entered her house by the back door.

Her mother was in the kitchen pressing one of her most becoming city frocks.

"Hello, Ginny," she said. "I'm glad you came home early. Your father just phoned. He was given four press tickets to that new play which opens in New York this evening. We've invited the Tryons and we're going to drive in and have dinner before the show." She carefully pulled the dress off the ironing board. "I hope you don't mind. Lila's still home with a cold. So hoarse she could hardly talk over the phone. But I fixed you a nice aspic out of leftovers. I thought you might invite Lucy over for dinner and to spend the night. We won't be back until after midnight."

"Of course, I don't mind," Ginny said. "Lucy and I'll have fun. Is there anything I can do to help you get ready?"

"You might brush my black coat," Mrs. Gordon said, hurrying up the stairs. "It's really too warm to wear now, but I'm going to anyway. That's how Lila

142

caught cold. Driving at night without her coat."

"I know," Ginny said. "It's hot when the sun is shining, but it gets cold at night. Joe Dakor told John that's how he got laryngitis. He drove up to Poughkeepsie Friday afternoon to look at some antiques, and, of course, it was so hot when he started out he wasn't dressed warmly enough."

"I'm sorry Joe is ill," Mrs. Gordon said absent-mindedly. "He's a nice boy."

"It seems to me a lot of people are hoarse," Ginny said as she vigorously brushed lint from her mother's coat. "I can't remember who else at the moment, but—" And then she did remember. Henderson's voice had been unpleasantly hoarse when he had threatened her. Whether it was normally gruff, she couldn't know. Instinctively she shivered, remembering that awful moment in the Barn when she realized that nobody could hear her if she had screamed.

"Why, what's the matter, Ginny?" Mrs. Gordon asked. "You look as though you'd seen a ghost!"

Ginny laughed. "A moth, maybe, but not a ghost."

"That's the trouble with this unseasonal heat," Mrs. Gordon said as Ginny helped her into her coat. "Moths thrive on it." She kissed Ginny good-by. "Your father is going to pick me up at the Tryons'. I'll give Lucy your invitation, if you like, and then you won't have to bother to phone."

"Thanks a lot," Ginny said. "The party lines are

always busy at this time of the afternoon."

Not long after Mrs. Gordon left the house, Lucy appeared, carrying an overnight bag and her books.

Ginny stared at her. "Why so formal? You've never bothered to bring anything but a toothbrush when you spent the night with me before."

Lucy laughed, rather nervously, Ginny thought. " 'Neither a borrower nor a lender be,' " she quoted.

"This Shakespeare bug," Ginny said, "must be catching. Which reminds me. I've got to dash over to the Reillys' for a while after supper. Whiz is going to give me some material for my English composition, in exchange for which I'm to try and explain to them that PRT means Principal times Rate times Time. You won't mind being alone, will you?"

"Oh, no," Lucy said. "I knew you had a date with the twins. I'll work on my own composition while you're gone."

"Fine," Ginny said and reached out for Lucy's overnight kit. "I'll take this upstairs and hang up your nightgown. I know how fussy and dainty you are."

Lucy hastily tried to snatch the handle away from Ginny. "Oh, no! Don't bother. I'll take it up myself."

Laughing, Ginny held on tightly. "I cawn't allow it, Gaston. You forget that you are my guest."

And then the bag burst open and a neatly folded

sheet fell out. Ginny's brown eyes were wide with surprise. "Why, Lucy Tryon," she gasped. "Do you mean to stand there and tell me that you brought sheets, too? What's come over you anyway?"

Lucy's plump cheeks were bright red one minute and then they paled. "I—I just thought," she stammered, "with Lila out sick, and washday yesterday, that maybe you wouldn't have any extra clean sheets."

"Oh," Ginny said in a relieved tone of voice. "That's different. In fact, it was very thoughtful of you. But we have plenty. You know how Mother is about bargains, Lucy. She simply can't resist Shoemaker's white sales. If I ever have a trousseau, I won't have to buy a thing."

"Like mother, like daughter," Lucy said, cramming the sheet back into her bag. "You can't resist bargains either, Ginny." She started up the stairs. "Don't bother to come up with me. I know my way around."

"You should," Ginny said, following her. "But I'm curious to see what else you brought. An electric blanket, by any chance?"

Lucy stopped on the landing. "Oh, Ginny, please, don't follow me as though you were afraid I was going to do something I shouldn't. It makes me nervous."

Ginny promptly turned around and skipped back down to the hall. "I'm sorry," she said gaily. "I was only teasing."

They studied a while and then they had supper. After they had washed and dried the dishes, Ginny said, "I may as well go over to the Reillys' now. Sure you won't be lonely?"

"Oh, no," Lucy assured her. "I've got lots of work to do."

Ginny slipped into her jacket and went out the back door. "I won't be gone more than half an hour," she called from the garage.

Lucy came out on the stoop. "It'll take longer than that to explain compound interest to the twins."

"Probably," Ginny said as she biked down the driveway. "I'll come back as soon as I can."

As it turned out, Whiz hadn't even looked for the Kentucky material he had promised Ginny, so it was almost eight when she put her bike back in the garage. She hurried into the house, calling, "Lucy, Lucy. Where are you?"

No answer. Ginny stood in the kitchen for a minute wondering where Lucy could have gone. "Probably forgot something and went home for it," she decided. "Although from the way her overnight bag bulged I'd have thought she brought everything but the kitchen stove."

Wearily Ginny climbed the stairs to her bedroom. She turned on the overhead light and then stood staring at the disheveled heap of clothes on the other twin bed. Lucy had evidently dumped the contents of her overnight kit on the counterpane, and that wasn't like Lucy. She was exceptionally dainty and hated to wear anything that was wrinkled.

Ginny moved over and extricated Lucy's nightgown and robe. She hung them in her closet and placed Lucy's mules on the floor. Not until then did she realize that there was no sign of the sheet which had fallen out of the bag earlier.

And suddenly Ginny thought she knew where Lucy was. *Oh, oh, oh,* she moaned as she dashed out of the house. *I should have guessed!*

Ginny ran as fast as she could down Main Street toward the Inn. *I haven't a chance of arriving in time to stop her,* she thought desperately. *They stop serving tea at six and they start serving dinner at eight. I only hope that I arrive in time to pick up the pieces!*

Gasping for breath, she raced up the Inn steps. The porch was empty, but the dining-room, she could see, was filled with older people.

There was no sign of Lochinvar, and no one was in the front hall when Ginny tore up the stairs, two at a time. On the second floor she stopped, completely out of breath. And then she saw them—Lochinvar and Lucy.

They were standing just outside the White Elephant, and Lucy was crying. Dangling from a rubber band on her wrist was a hideous Halloween mask and she was standing ankle-deep in the folds of a crumpled sheet.

Ginny took a deep breath. The worst had happened. Neither of them had seen her yet, and she sank down on the top step to try and decide what she could do to get Lucy out of this scrape.

"But you don't understand," she heard Lucy sob. "Ginny's my very best friend. She's so terribly disappointed, and the boys worked so hard."

Lochinvar, whose back was turned to Ginny, said, "I couldn't noways think of turnen you over to the powleece. I jist don't onderstand. I allus liked young-uns, but 'pears like you young-uns don't like me."

"It isn't that," Lucy wailed. "We think you're just wonderful, too wonderful, in fact. If only you'd go away."

"I hain't liable to take my foot in my hand and go nowhere," Lochinvar said, "ontell I git some explanation of why you come a-traipsen around here rigged up like a hant. I'm plumb tuckered out with outlandishest doens. Fust you make off with my accordion. Then you haf drownded me. Atter that you let the air out o' my tires. Atter that you writ me a contrarious letter, and 'fore I kin figger out what hit all means, you jump out at me, holleren fit to wake the dead."

"I didn't," Lucy sobbed. "I didn't do all those things to you. I just dressed up like a ghost and hid

"If Only You'd Go Away!" Lucy Wailed

in the rest room. Then when you started out of your room I came out into the hall and said, 'OOOh, whoo!' That's all I did. I—I thought it might scare you into leaving town."

Ginny jumped to her feet. "I can explain everything, Mr. Lochinvar," she said.

He turned to face her with a startled expression on his face. "You here, too?" He clutched his thick black hair with both hands. "I hain't hardly equal to hit."

He looked so completely baffled that Ginny had to suppress a smile. "I'm terribly sorry, Mr. Lochinvar," she said, moving down the hall to Lucy's side. "It's really all my fault. I got weepy yesterday when I had to face the fact that the Barn is a dismal failure. And Lucy thought she was doing something helpful when she draped herself in that sheet and covered her face with this silly mask. It's really very easy to explain," she went on hurriedly as the expression on his face grew more amazed. "I meant to come over here and apologize soon anyway, but what with the sandwiches and the can opener and the peanut butter, and then the glue and John's nice pine board all disappearing—"

"Don't forget the shrimp and the cream cheese and pineapple," Lucy added nervously. "We're all going crazy, Mr. Lochinvar. And it started with blank sheets of paper in blank envelopes, so you really shouldn't be cross."

He backed away from them, still clutching his hair wildly. "No more sech talk," he implored. "You two is mighty flighty girl-chilluns, I'll be bound."

"Be quiet," Ginny hissed to Lucy. "Let me explain. You're only making things worse."

"Nothen could be wusser than this," he said, covering his face with his hands. "I cain't ricoleck anythen like this ever happenen to me before."

"Oh, dear," Ginny moaned hopelessly. "Can't we go someplace and talk quietly? I know they're all waiting for you down in the dining-room, Mr. Lochinvar, but this is really important. You've simply got to understand about the Snack Barn. It explains everything. Even the silly things Babs did, although I must say, what Lucy did was just as silly. If she knew as much as I know now about Kentucky mountaineers she wouldn't have done it. Only the old, *old* people still believe in the devil and witches and ghosts. And very few people who can read and write still talk in the dialect."

Slowly he uncovered his face. "Then you don't think I'm a real hillbilly?" he asked.

"No, I don't," Ginny said stanchly. "But I love the way you talk, although it confuses me at times."

He burst into gales of laughter. "Has anyone ever told you, Ginny Gordon, that the way *you* talk is confusing at times?"

Ginny joined in his laughter. "I'm famous for talking too fast and for trying to say too much in one breath." She stared up at him. "Then you aren't a real hillbilly?"

He shrugged his broad shoulders. "That depends upon your definition. I was born and reared in the Cumberland Mountains, but I also happen to be a college graduate." He bent down to whisper to the girls. "That has got to be our secret. Mr. Crayne might fire me if word got around that I can speak English better than a lot of his customers."

"We won't tell a soul," Ginny promised. "But don't you worry, Mr. Crayne wouldn't fire you even if you had several college degrees."

Lochinvar drew back with a startled expression on his face. "What made you say that?"

"Oh, for goodness sake, Mr. Lochinvar," Lucy cried impatiently. "You shouldn't be so modest. You must know that you're simply super and that's why we want you to leave town." She tossed her blond bob defiantly. "If I thought it would do any good to tell Mr. Crayne on you, I would. Think of what you've cost us, almost five hundred dollars! Unless Mrs. Arnold crashes through, and has Betty and Carson's wedding reception there. But even that won't save us." She crumpled down on the carpet and buried her face in the sheet. "If every child in this town turns out to be a wayward minor it's all your fault, Mr. Lochinvar."

Instantly he was on his knees beside her. "There, there, honey," he said soothingly. "You keep forgetting that I don't know what crime I've committed."

A bellhop appeared at the top of the stairs then. "You'd better scram down to the dinner crowd, Lochinvar," he said. "The manager is on the verge of apoplexy."

The tall singer drew himself up to his full height. "Scram yourself," he said coldly, and then added hastily, "I'd be mighty grateful if you'd take the trouble to remind Mistuh Crayne that I did a bit o' ovahtime Satiddy night. If the gennelman ricolecks, he'll call to mind that he owes me a passel o' pay-money." He bowed the bellhop away and turned to Ginny. "Have you girls got a home where we could go and talk this thing out in peace? All I've heard you mention so far is a barn."

Ginny giggled. "It would be simply wonderful if you'd come home and have a long talk with us, Mr. Lochinvar."

"Let's go," he said, helping Lucy to her feet. "And leave out the mister, please." He crooked his elbows at them. "Slip your arms through mine. We can sneak out the back way to the parking lot. I've done it before."

Ginny carefully chose his left arm. As they dashed down the stairs she brushed against him and knew that she had not imagined that he carried a pistol in a shoulder holster.

He vaulted into his jeep as agilely as a cat, and they climbed into the seat beside him. He cocked an eyebrow at Ginny. "Where to?"

"Down Main to Maple," she said. "Turn left on Maple. Our driveway is the fourth on the right."

Ten minutes later they were all settled comfortably in the Gordons' cozy library. Then Ginny, talking slowly and carefully, explained about the Snack Barn.

"Well, if that isn't something," he said when she had finished. "If only I'd known on Saturday! But it still isn't too late." He grinned across the desk at Ginny. "Don't waste a penny putting an ad in your father's paper. As of snack time tomorrow, I'll be singing at the Barn."

Ginny and Lucy gasped. "But how?" they said in one voice.

"Simple," he told them, waving his hands airily. "Mr. Crayne is none too happy about the half dollars he collects from your schoolmates who sit around all afternoon. And Officer Bill is quite right. The Inn isn't the place for youngsters. They should spend their leisure time at the Barn, and if I have anything to do with it, they shall from now on!"

CHAPTER TWELVE

NIGHT VISITORS

It all seemed too good to be true! The Harristown pied piper was going to draw the teen-age crowd away from the Inn and back to the Barn.

And then Ginny was struck with a thought that plunged her into the depths of despair. "But, Lochinvar," she said, sadly shaking her head. "We can't afford to pay you a salary."

"Think nothing of that," he said cheerily. "We'll do it on a percentage of profit basis. I get one per cent, you get ninety-nine. Does that strike you as fair?"

"Much more than fair," Ginny said worriedly. "I can't consider it, unless you take twenty-five per cent." She leaned forward to ask him very seriously, "Why don't you go into television or the movies, Lochinvar? You'd make a mint."

He shrugged and sang Gilbert and Sullivan's famous melody, " 'A wandering minstrel, I!' " Then he chuckled. "I'll bet that during the past month I've visited more cities and towns on the East Coast than even you smart girls ever heard of. I like to travel."

"It must be fun being a wandering minstrel,"

Ginny said thoughtfully. "Whenever you get sick and tired of a place, you simply pack up your accordion and move on."

"That's right," he said. "In spite of my college education, I guess I'm a tramp."

Lucy giggled. "I always said you were a vagrant. In fact," she confessed, "I even asked Officer Bill to pick you up and make you leave town. After first putting you in jail for awhile."

At that the big, handsome singer collapsed with laughter. "You kids certainly were anxious to get rid of me," he choked. "And I don't blame you. But don't worry, I'll make it all up to you." He unfolded his long legs. "Better stock up on snack materials when you leave school tomorrow."

"We will," Ginny assured him as she walked to the front door with him. "But how will the kids know you're not going to be at the Inn?"

"I'll take care of that," he said. "There'll be a big sign at the bicycle stand announcing that I will be at the Snack Barn from now on whenever you're open for business."

"Oh, wonderful," Ginny cried. "Even Saturday lunches and Sunday brunches? Won't Mr. Crayne object?"

"I'm sure he won't," Lochinvar said. "The big spenders are the dinner and week-end supper crowds. I'll make a deal with him that will make him much happier than he is now." He shook his head, smiling. "I like kids, but they *were* wrecking the place. Mr. Crayne was thinking of keeping them away with a big cover charge, but that might well have hurt his adult business."

Ginny laughed. "What's a drop in the bucket to the Inn is a small fortune to us. We could use a lot of fifty centses right now."

He nodded understandingly. "For that oil burner? I wish I thought I were going to be around long enough to make sure you get it, but I'm afraid I won't."

"Oh, dear," Lucy wailed. "You can't leave soon. You just can't!"

He grinned down at her. "Not long ago you were trying to get rid of me! If I don't watch my step, you'll be getting your policeman friend to lock me up so you can keep me here."

Ginny followed him out on the porch. "No," she said thoughtfully. "I really wouldn't want you to stay very long, Lochinvar, even though I think you're the grandest man in the world next to my father. You see, as long as you're the drawing card, we'll never know whether or not the Snack Barn is a success in itself. We planned it to be a place where our schoolmates could entertain themselves and each other. What I'm trying to say," she went on seriously, "is that we wanted them to feel that it was theirs as much as ours. If you can just get them into the habit of coming there, they'll keep coming and soon it'll be the community project we hoped it would be."

He had started down the steps toward his jeep, but he turned to look up at her. "You're a very wise young lady, Ginny Gordon," he said. "If every town in America had a teen-age Snack Barn, there would be fewer criminals in the world!"

The girls waved good-by to him and then hurried upstairs to get ready for bed. "Thish hash beeth the mosh citish b-day in my lifesh," Lucy spluttered as she brushed her teeth.

"Mine, too," Ginny said, vigorously brushing her short chestnut curls.

"Donsh talsk wish your head upside down," Lucy said. "I can't understand you."

Ginny perched on the edge of the bathtub. "You're the limit, Lucy," she said. "Only *I* could understand you when your mouth is full of tooth-paste. And you have the nerve—"

"Never mind," Lucy said, doubling over to brush her own back hair. "If it hadn't been for me, Loch-invar wouldn't be on our side. I'm glad I thought of dressing up like a ghost. But it was a terrifying moment when he grabbed me, and the sheet and mask fell off."

"You're talking through a mask of long yellow hair right now," Ginny pointed out. "Let's go to bed, then you can start at the beginning and tell me everything that happened."

In a few minutes they were snuggling under the covers on the twin beds in Ginny's room. "Fate," Ginny said, "seems to play into the hands of blondes as well as redheads. If Dad hadn't got those passes to the opening in New York, you wouldn't have spent the night with me, and even if you had, with my parents home, you couldn't have sneaked out and gone to the Inn when you did."

"I know," Lucy admitted. "I planned to rig up some sort of a ghostly contraption that would jiggle up and down when he opened the door of the White Elephant to go down and sing during dinner. Babs's booby trap gave me the idea. But then when your mother said I was invited to spend the night, and I knew you were going to coach the Reillys in compound interest, I decided to play ghost myself."

"You mean booby," Ginny said with a sniff. "I don't know why Lochinvar didn't grab you and shake the living daylights out of you when you whoo-whooed at him."

"He did shake me," Lucy said with a giggle. "Just once. But once was enough. Both the mask and sheet slipped, so I was blinded and practically hobbled. The next thing I knew I was sprawling headlong at his feet." She giggled more loudly. "He helped me untangle myself and said a lot of angry words in that Kentucky dialect which I couldn't understand, so I thought the best thing to do was to tell him that *he* didn't understand."

"That's where I came in," Ginny said, reaching out to switch off the lamp on the table between the beds. "Luckily for you and Babs," she went on sternly, "Lochinvar obviously doesn't believe in turning wayward minors over to the police."

"One thing you're right about," Lucy said sleepily, "is that he does carry a pistol in a shoulder holster."

"How do you know?" Ginny demanded.

"Because," Lucy told her, "when I first jumped out at him, his right arm went to the left side of his shirt as quick as a flash. And then, just as quickly, it was clamped around my own right arm. I tell you, Ginny, that man moves so fast he must have had training in jujitsu."

"I think you're right," Ginny said. "When we dashed down the back stairs of the Inn, hanging on to his arms, it was the same thing as descending in a parachute. My feet never touched the floor once, did yours?"

But Lucy was sound asleep. Ginny herself fell asleep in another minute to dream that Lochinvar did indeed have wings and flew into the Barn singing in a disagreeably hoarse voice.

She awoke long before dawn and began at once to plan for the thrilling day that lay ahead of her and the other Hustlers. How surprised they would be when they heard the good news! Ginny knew that she couldn't sleep another wink, so she dressed quiet-

ly and went down into the kitchen. It was growing
light by the time she finished eating a quick breakfast of cereal, milk, and fruit juice, and it suddenly
occurred to her that she had plenty of time in which
to bike out to the Barn and still get back in time
for school.

"I'll make as many sandwiches as I can," she decided. "It's going to be hectic trying to keep up with
the crowd that'll surely be there this afternoon. As
it is, Lucy and I will have to waste a lot of time buying supplies when we get out of school."

Ginny peeked into her mother's bread box and
discovered to her delight that it contained two extra
loaves of fresh bread. "I'll just leave enough for
breakfast toast," she decided, hurrying out to the
garage. "Mother won't mind when she reads the
note I left explaining."

The air was chilly and damp as she biked through
the park and Ginny wished that she had slipped on
her jacket before leaving the house. By pedaling as
fast as she could she soon warmed up and was almost
too hot by the time she reached the Barn. Then she
saw that the bow of the padlock had not been
snapped in place.

"That Whiz," she muttered crossly. "I suppose
John left yesterday before he did and told him to
lock up. But instead, he simply hung the bow from
the staple and forgot to snap it."

There was no sense in wasting time rehearsing the

scolding she was going to give Whiz when she met him in the cafeteria at noon. There was too much to do.

Ginny scrubbed her hands at the sink and opened the refrigerator door, planning to make the first batch of sandwiches out of the jar of spread John had opened with his knife yesterday.

But the jar was gone and so was a stick of butter. Ginny almost burst into tears. She had biked all the way out here for nothing, for without a can opener or a sharp-pointed knife she couldn't open a thing. Then she remembered that there were plenty of eggs, lettuce and mayonnaise.

"Egg salad sandwiches will be just the thing," she decided. "I can wash and dry the lettuce and spread butter on slices of bread while the eggs are boiling."

Ginny set a small pan of water on one of the burners and took the carton of eggs out of the refrigerator. In it were eight eggs instead of the twelve she and Lucy had bought yesterday.

"I could shake Whiz until his teeth rattle," she mumbled. "He keeps saying that tramps don't come into locked barns and then he carefully leaves our Barn unlocked. I wonder what else is missing."

A quick glance in the cupboard showed her that nothing had been taken from the shelves except the can of tuna fish Babs had wanted to open yesterday.

Ginny sat on the stool to think while the eggs boiled. The person who had robbed them the third time either had a can opener of his own, or else he was the same person who had stolen theirs. She tried to remember everything she had heard or read about tramps. A mental picture came to her mind of ragged men in a hobo jungle using forked sticks to heat open cans of food over a fire. Tramps apparently didn't bother to carry pots and pans with them, but they obviously traveled with can openers.

"Then why did one of them steal ours?" she asked herself. She knew what John would reply with that slow smile of his: "Just because all chairs are furniture doesn't mean that every piece of furniture is a chair." In other words, most tramps probably carried can openers, but not all tramps carried them all the time.

Ginny washed the lettuce and shook the leaves dry in a towel. "I don't care what anybody says," she muttered. "I don't think tramps have been stealing our supplies. *I* think someone is playing mean tricks on us because he feels the same way about us that Babs and Lucy did about Lochinvar. Whoever it is wants to make us leave the Barn."

By the time Ginny finished making all the sandwiches she could, she had decided not to discuss the third robbery with the other Hustlers. A lot of valuable time would be wasted while each one presented his or her theory, and Whiz would be sure to do a lot of clowning. Today of all days, everyone must be serious and efficient.

Quickly Ginny made a list of the supplies they would need. "Five dollars will never be enough," she realized. "Besides, I owe Mother for what we charged to her account yesterday. I'd better get our pass book from the cash box and take some more money out of the bank during my lunch hour."

She reached down to the shelf where they kept the cash box, and lifted it up to the counter. Then she saw to her surprise that although she had not locked the box and had left the key in the lock, the box was now locked and the key was missing.

"John," she moaned. "It must have been John, he's so careful. And actually, I shouldn't have left the box unlocked with the bank book in it, because if anyone should swipe that we *would* be ruined."

At the same moment she realized that without the identifying pass book, she couldn't draw a cent out of the bank. Ginny glanced at her wrist watch. It was eight-fifteen and the first bell rang at eight-forty-five. She couldn't possibly bike in to John's for the key and back again without being late to school. Neither would there be time during the lunch hour for a round trip and a visit to the bank. And the bank closed at three o'clock.

"But we've got to have some more money," Ginny wailed. "I'll just have to lug this heavy old box into town and leave it at home when I pick up my books. The way things are developing now, I guess I won't have time for a bite of lunch. What with getting the key from John, then going home for the bank book, and finally standing in line at the bank, I'll be lucky if I don't miss the first afternoon class."

Suddenly she remembered that before they had had a duplicate key made, when they were all forever needing money for this or that, they had kept the key way back on the shelf. John just might have put Ginny's key there yesterday afternoon.

Without much hope she stooped and reached back as far as she could. The sleeve of her sweater knocked something to the floor. It was the key to the cash box.

"Well, I never!" she exploded. "I can't imagine why John went to all the trouble of locking the box and then left the key on the shelf in *front* of it."

That wasn't like careful John, and Ginny stood there for a moment staring at the key and trying to figure out why he hadn't put it in the old hiding place. Then it dawned on her that John's carefulness was the answer. If he were delayed with both keys in his pocket, no one could open the box. So he had left hers in a place where she would be sure to find it, but where a stranger would probably never think of looking.

Ginny unlocked the box and lifted the lid. Then she let out a little scream of surprise. For, lying on top of the empty change compartments was a long, white envelope. Printed on it in pencil were two words: *Mr. Chadwell.*

CHAPTER THIRTEEN

THE LONG, WHITE ENVELOPE

Ginny was so surprised that she staggered back and collapsed on the stool. She must be dreaming. There couldn't be an envelope in the cash box addressed to Mr. Chadwell. She rubbed her eyes and looked again.

There it was, there wasn't any doubt about it. Gingerly Ginny picked up the envelope and stared at the name. Then she turned it over and saw that it was sealed. Whoever had sealed it had pretty grimy hands, for the flap was smeared and soiled.

"I don't care if it is sealed," Ginny said to herself. "I've got to know what's in this envelope before I go to school or I'll fail in every subject."

She switched on the light over the sink and held the envelope close to the bulb. A one-thousand-dollar bill showed plainly through the cheap paper! Ginny's hands were trembling with excitement as she turned the envelope and held the other side against the bulb. Another thousand-dollar bill! Deftly she gauged the thickness of the envelope's contents.

"This is it," she gasped. "Unless I'm dreaming there are five one-thousand-dollar bills in this dirty envelope. What on earth am I going to do with them?"

A quick glance at her wrist watch told her that if she didn't leave at once she would be late to school. She couldn't leave that much money in the cash box. It had already been proved that anyone could break into it by simply prying off the hinges.

Clutching the envelope and the pass book, Ginny hurried out, snapped the padlock bow and got on her bike. She would have to figure out the answer to this new problem on her way home.

John would, of course, say that the money must be deposited to their account in the bank for safe-keeping. Ginny could think of two strong objections to that. Depositing such a large sum would be sure to cause a lot of embarrassing questions from adults.

"Where on earth did you get all that money?"

"Five one-thousand-dollar bills! What are you kids up to?"

No, that was not the answer. Besides, Chadwell would be sure to show up and demand the money any day now. For it must have been Henderson who put it in the box. Henderson, Ginny reasoned, after stealing the envelope addressed to him, must have had a change of heart and decided to live up to the terms of the bargain. When he returned to the Barn he found everything conveniently set up for him; the padlock unsnapped and the cash box unlocked. So he simply put the envelope in the box, locked the box and left the key on the shelf in front of it. His next step would be to notify Chadwell that the deal had gone through as agreed: Five one-thousand-dollar bills were waiting for him at the Snack Barn.

Suppose Chadwell appeared this very afternoon? If Ginny deposited the money in the bank at noon, he would have to wait another day. Ginny, herself, had no desire to postpone the end of the whole complicated, confusing business. She wanted to wash her hands of it. And that meant that she must have the money with her whenever she went to the Barn.

"I'll clip the envelope to one of the pages of notes I've taken for my English composition," she decided finally. "And I'll never take those pages out of my looseleaf notebook—not until Chadwell shows up."

Lucy, with both sets of schoolbooks, was waiting for her by Ginny's front steps.

"I thought you'd never come back," she said, dumping Ginny's books in her bike basket. "What on earth made you go out to the Barn at the crack of dawn, and what is that big envelope you're clutching?"

Ginny quickly made up her mind to tell Lucy what had happened, but nobody else. She stopped long enough to slip the envelope and the bank book inside her looseleaf binder, then they both pedaled furiously toward school.

"The envelope," Ginny told Lucy, "is addressed to Mr. Chadwell and it's full of thousand-dollar bills.

I found it in the cash box."

Lucy gasped. "But how—what—?"

"I'll tell you all about it," Ginny said, "if you'll come to the bank with me after lunch while I draw out some money."

"Draw *out* some money?" Lucy demanded. "You aren't going to keep those thousand-dollar bills in your notebook, are you?"

"I certainly am," Ginny said firmly. "They'll be perfectly safe there. And you're not to tell a soul that I have them. Especially not John and Babs. Babs can't keep secrets and John would make me put it in the bank."

"I won't tell anybody," Lucy said. "If for no other reason than that I'm afraid you'd get bopped on the head. Why, Ginny, people have committed murder for less than that."

"Don't be silly," Ginny said as they hurried up the steps of the school. "Nobody's going to bop me on the head. Chadwell will probably show up this afternoon or tomorrow and I'll simply give him the envelope with my blessing."

"If I were you," Lucy said, "I'd demand an explanation. Why didn't he come back when he said he would and why didn't Henderson do what he was supposed to do?" She stopped halfway up the steps. "Did that fat man break in through a window again?"

"He didn't have to this time," Ginny said. "Whiz

didn't snap the padlock."

"I know he didn't," Lucy said, surprised. "But John did. I saw him. He snapped it and then he tested it. He said he was afraid that since the lock was picked the tumblers or something might not work properly."

"Then," Ginny said, "the lock was picked again. And whoever did it, left in such a hurry he didn't snap the bow in place."

"Oh, Ginny," Lucy cried. *"You're* why he left in such a hurry. He must have been inside the Barn when you turned into the lane from the highway and he saw you from one of the windows." She shuddered. "You shouldn't have disobeyed John, Ginny. He laid down the law about us not going out there without one of the boys."

The first bell rang then and they hurried off to their home room. Not until they were standing at the end of the long line outside the cashier's window did the girls have a chance to talk again.

"I've been thinking," Ginny said. "Two people must have been in the Barn last night. Our lock-picking tramp who swiped some more food—and Henderson. The tramp must have left in a hurry when he heard Henderson coming along the lane. That's why the padlock wasn't snapped."

"I guess you're right," Lucy said. "People who don't mind leaving five thousand dollars in un-burglar-proof cash boxes, don't swipe food. What was taken this time?"

"Nothing very vital," Ginny said. "But it's getting to be a nuisance. I had to hardboil eggs this morning for sandwiches instead of simply using the stuff in the jar John opened yesterday. I was so mad for a minute I almost burst into tears."

Lucy nodded sympathetically. "I really think, Ginny," she said, "that we ought to report the thefts to Officer Bill. Especially since you're going to ask the grocer to deliver about twelve dollars' worth of stuff today. Why, suppose some dishonest person with a trailer happened along! We could be cleaned out overnight!"

Ginny laughed. "What I'm hoping is that we'll be cleaned out over-afternoon, and every afternoon while Lochinvar is here." She sobered. "You're right, Lucy. We can't spare the time to shop except for fresh bread and things like that after school from now on. We'll have to keep well-stocked because the gang will arrive at about the same time that we get there. I'd better buy about thirty dollars' worth of stuff today and ask Mr. Jones to have it all delivered at three-thirty."

"That's what I think," Lucy said worriedly. "We've got enough stuff for quite a lot of cheeseburgers in case he's late. I'm glad now that you were so optimistic yesterday. But," she went on, "I won't sleep nights knowing that there's nothing but that silly padlock between a tramp and so much of our investment."

"It's awful," Ginny agreed, "but I simply can't talk to Officer Bill now. If we tell him anything we'll have to tell him everything. And then the fact that I have five thousand dollars in this notebook will come out. I don't have to tell you what the result of that will be."

"I know all too well," Lucy said. "You'll get the dickens for having anything to do with Mr. Chadwell's weird proposal in the first place; and, in the second place, it's going to be hard to explain to your father why you kept it a secret for so long."

"I wish I hadn't now," Ginny admitted. "I wish I'd told Dad about it in the very beginning. It seems to me that I'm always getting into scrapes and then regretting too late that I kept secrets from my parents."

"Truer words were never spoken," Lucy said with a chuckle. "Although actually, Ginny, I don't blame you for not telling your parents about that first envelope. It didn't make any sense. But this thieving business has got to be stopped."

"I know it," Ginny said. "And it's all my fault we can't report it to Officer Bill. If it hadn't been for me the rest of you would have told him when we found those sandwiches were missing."

"Don't feel badly about it," Lucy cried impulsively. "You know what I think you ought to do? I think you ought to ask Lochinvar's advice. That

man's smart. You can tell from the way he talks that
he knows a lot about a lot of things. And I don't
mean just because he's a college graduate either."

"I know just what you mean," Ginny said. "And
the first chance I get, I will ask his advice. I'll tell
him everything except about the money. Nobody,
but *nobody*, Lucy, must know about that until after
I've turned it over to Chadwell."

They were nearing the cashier's window now and
Lucy said, "I'll run over to the hardware store and
get one of those can openers the boys can attach to
the wall. They're much better than the cheaper kind
and of absolutely no use to a tramp."

During lunch in the cafeteria, the girls had told
the twins and John the good news. Once Lucy had
almost blurted out that Lochinvar spoke better English than most people, but Ginny had kicked her
under the table just in time.

Now Ginny was afraid that Lucy might let another cat out of the bag. Ginny knew how fast gossip
traveled in a small suburb; and she also knew that
people had committed serious crimes for less than
five thousand dollars. As she walked back to school
she passed the *News* building and gazed up at its
windows. If only she could run in and tell her father
the whole story. Then she could turn the money
over to him and forget about the puzzling affair.

"I'll never feel safe again until I get rid of it," she
thought. "But maybe Chadwell will show up today.

I certainly hope so."

But Ginny hoped in vain. However, Lochinvar's
initial appearance at the Barn was so successful that
she had no time to worry about the envelope in her
loose-leaf notebook under the counter. By four
o'clock in the afternoon, every boy and girl in Harristown who could, came to the Barn. The room was
packed and jammed with a hilariously happy and
hungry crowd. Lochinvar seemed to be enjoying
himself as much as anyone. He sang and played
every song anyone requested, and insisted upon
everyone joining in the chorus.

"This is so much more fun than the Inn," Ginny's
classmates told her over and over again. "How did
you ever wangle it?"

They never seemed to tire of hearing vivid de-
scriptions of Babs's and Lucy's escapades which had
culminated in Lochinvar's transfer to the Barn. And,
to Ginny's satisfaction, when Lochinvar left at five-
thirty in order to rest his voice before entertaining
at the Inn later, the crowd stayed on.

"We can't serve food after five-thirty," Ginny said
firmly when Whiz's classmates clamored for more
cheeseburgers. "It'll ruin your appetite for dinner."

"Only singing waiters," Whiz said, "are allowed
to eat after the official closing time. Rustle up some
grub for me, girls."

"We'll do nothing of the kind," Lucy said. "It's

Lochinvar Played All the Songs They Requested

yours and Babs's turn to wash the dishes. You'd better get going if you expect to be home in time for supper."

With everyone helping, the Barn was spick-and-span by the time the last customer left. Then Ginny announced:

"We took in almost fifteen dollars, which is pretty good considering the time limit. We should double it on Saturdays and Sundays, which means that our profit will be about fifty dollars a week. Twenty-five per cent of it goes to Lochinvar."

"Holy smoke," Whiz interrupted. "Do you mean that guy is going to work for us for a measly twelve or fifteen dollars a week? He's demented."

"Kind-hearted is the word," Ginny corrected him. "He only wanted to take one percent in the beginning. Anyway, if things keep on the way they started, we should have in the bank by Christmas our original five-hundred-dollar investment."

John nodded thoughtfully. "I can see what you're driving at, Ginny. Do we hang on until we get back what we put into it, or do we turn it over to the community as soon as the town fathers decide that it should be a Youth Center?"

"Great grizzly bears," Babs moaned. "It seems to me that we're always starting things which we give away as soon as they get going."

"We didn't exactly give away the Swap Shop," Whiz reminded her. "Five hundred smackers was a neat sum just for our good will."

"And running a restaurant," Ginny went on, "is a lot harder than I thought it would be. The Health Department laws and all this worry about tramps. If this Barn had the police force behind it, no one would dare break in."

"And," Lucy added, "the constant worry about how much to buy. It drives me crazy trying to figure out whether we should buy five loaves of bread or two."

"The oil burner," Whiz put in, "will cost a pretty penny, not to mention the fact that we'll have to have a storage tank which we'll have to remember to keep filled."

"It sounds more complicated by the minute," Babs said. "Besides, when business is good, I don't get a chance to eat anything. And whenever there's anything left over, tramps eat it."

John looked at Ginny with a puzzled expression on his face. "Have we been robbed again?"

Ginny nodded. "I found a few things missing when I came out here this morning. I blamed it on Whiz because the bow of the padlock wasn't snapped. But Lucy says you did snap it, John."

"I certainly did." He got up and went outside to inspect the lock. They all followed him. "It works all right," he told them. "Someone picked it again, that's all."

"That's all," Lucy repeated with a sniff. "I think

we ought to report the thefts to Officer Bill. They're getting on my nerves."

"Don't be silly," Ginny said quickly. "What on earth can Officer Bill do to keep tramps away? He'll simply say that we should have a burglar-proof lock installed on the door, and that would cost a mint."

"Good ones run into money," Whiz agreed. "Another answer Officer Bill can give if we complain about the tramps is that we should employ a night watchman, which is out of the question."

"That's right," Ginny said. "So what's the use of complaining? It's a problem we'll have to solve ourselves."

"But how?" Lucy demanded. "I didn't worry when we had such a few supplies on hand, but now that we're well-stocked, it gives me the jitters thinking about what might happen."

"We can't stand around here talking about it any longer," Ginny said. "We'll be late to dinner. Let's go."

She put her books and the cracker can of money in her basket and biked off. By the time she reached her home she had made up her mind. Tramps had not been breaking into the Barn to steal food. All three thefts had been committed by the same person, and that person had to be someone who couldn't get food any other way.

Someone, Ginny felt sure, was hiding out in the woods; someone who was wanted by the police.

CHAPTER FOURTEEN

CLUES AND A COMPOSITION

Ginny did her homework that evening as fast as she could. Then she settled down to list her clues. She opened her loose-leaf binder to the blank pages in the back and wrote:

(1) Tramps don't usually break into locked barns.

(2) Tramps don't usually stay in one place very long.

(3) Tramps usually avoid Harristown.

(4) It's too much of a coincidence to think that three different tramps, three nights in succession, broke into the Barn.

(5) Nothing was stolen from us except food.

(6) People who need food but have no use for money are people who can't go to stores and buy food.

(7) People who avoid public places are usually people who are wanted by the police.

(8) Therefore, the person who has been breaking into the Barn is wanted by the police. And he must be hiding out in the woods.

Ginny slowly read what she had written. Then she shook her head. If she gave Officer Bill this sheet of paper he would only make fun of her. He would say that she was letting her imagination run away with her. She could almost hear him say,

"You kids and your vagrants. You'll be the death of me yet."

Ginny turned the paper over and began to write on the other side:

(1) I think Chadwell is wanted by the police. That's why he hasn't come back for his money. Officer Bill has been there almost every day since we opened.

(2) I think Chadwell is a blackmailer.

(3) Henderson is his victim.

(4) Chadwell has letters which are worth five thousand dollars to Henderson. He agreed to meet Chadwell somewhere and give him the money for the letters.

(5) Chadwell is wanted by the police and so they couldn't meet in a public place. They decided that the Snack Barn, run by teen-agers, would be a very safe place.

(6) Chadwell planned to doublecross Henderson. He gave me blank stationery instead of the letters. He felt sure Henderson would give me the money first and examine the contents of the envelope later.

(7) When Henderson arrived and found me there alone he realized that he might be able to get the letters without paying me a cent. He tried to

make me give them to him, and finally broke into the Barn and took the envelope out of the cash box.

(8) Later he realized that Chadwell had tried to doublecross him. But he still has to get the letters.

(9) He can't get in touch with Chadwell because Chadwell is hiding from the police.

(10) His only chance is that Chadwell will eventually return to the Barn. If the money is there, Chadwell may give me the letters for it.

(11) So Henderson sneaked into the Barn last night and put the money in the cash box.

(12) Chadwell, a burglar as well as a blackmailer, has been hiding out in the woods.

(13) He couldn't come into the Barn on Sunday morning as he promised because Officer Bill was there.

(14) On Sunday night he picked the padlock and the cash box lock. The envelope he had addressed to Henderson was still there. So he took the sandwiches and went back to his hiding place. Later Henderson broke in and stole the envelope.

(15) On Monday night Chadwell again picked the locks hoping he would find that the envelope he had addressed to Henderson was gone, and that in its place would be one for him from Henderson containing five thousand dollars. There was nothing in the box but our petty cash, so he stole some more food and left.

(16) He broke in again last night to find the cash

box empty. He took some more food, and then he heard someone coming along the lane. He left in such a hurry he didn't snap the bow of the padlock.

(17) The person he heard was Henderson who put the money in the cash box, locked it, and left.

By this time Ginny had covered two sheets of paper and she carefully read what she had written. It all made sense to her, but she knew that John and Lucy would call her reasoning fantastic. And as for Officer Bill—he would howl with laughter. So would Whiz.

But Ginny was convinced that Chadwell was a criminal and that he was hiding out in the woods. "He'll keep sneaking into the Barn every night," she decided, "until he gives up or gets the money. He doesn't dare ask me for it in the daytime for fear Officer Bill may arrive while he's there."

One sure way to stop the thefts was to leave the envelope addressed to Chadwell in the cash box overnight. "And that," Ginny told herself, "I'll never do. Somehow I've got to prove that he's a criminal and then Officer Bill can stay out there one night and catch him."

Ginny knew that the fingerprints of all known criminals were on file in the Identification Division of the FBI in Washington. With his various powders and chemicals, Whiz could probably find prints on the cash box which did not belong to any of the Hustlers. But how could they convince Officer Bill that photographs of those prints should be sent to Washington?

And then Ginny had an idea. If Chadwell were wanted by any law enforcement agency, Officer Bill must have seen photographs of him. Somehow she would rig up a booby trap with her camera. A booby trap which would mean that the next time Chadwell sneaked into the Barn he would take his own picture. When the print was developed she would have something to show Officer Bill which would prove that her theory was correct.

Ginny had no idea how to set up such a trap. She would have to get the information from the boys without letting them know what she planned to do. And the next day something happened which she thought would make it easy for her to get the information she wanted.

When they biked out from school they found Lochinvar waiting for them in his jeep which he had parked beside the Barn.

"Your jeep and our bikes," John said, smiling, "are the only vehicles in town which can climb this lane."

Lochinvar grinned. "I ought to get a bike. They're not so noisy. I frightened away your pet pheasants when I arrived."

"Pet pheasants?" Ginny asked. "We haven't any."

"You may not know it, but you have," he told her. "I flushed two beauties. They were right here by the door and I imagine stuffing their crops with crumbs."

"Don't tell Officer Bill," Lucy said worriedly. "Crumbs are probably a violation of some law."

"No, a few crumbs are permissible," he told her. "And the Fish and Wildlife Service would heartily approve of your feeding pheasants."

"I'd like to see them," Ginny said as they trooped indoors. "But I guess they fly into the woods when they hear us coming. Wouldn't it be fun," she went on shrewdly, "if we could get pictures of them?"

"Don't be ridic," Babs said, "we couldn't get that near them."

"You don't have to," Ginny retorted. "Famous writers who only hunt with cameras, are always getting wonderful pictures of lions and tigers without getting near them." She turned to John. "How do they do it anyway?"

"Ask Whiz," he said. "He's the electrical genius. I hope the iceman shows up when he promised. I ordered another hundred pounds. The piece he brought yesterday is just about melted."

"It's the weather," Ginny said. "But it's an ill wind that blows no good. Ice is cheaper than fuel oil." She turned to Whiz. "How do they do it?"

"How do they do what?" he demanded.

"Booby traps for animals," Ginny said. "How would you go about rigging up one so that the pheasants would take their own pictures without knowing it, Whiz?"

But Whiz was paying no attention. He was staring at Lochinvar. "Say," he said suspiciously. "A minute ago you weren't talking like a hillbilly. You were talking like a guy who—who—"

"Had a little education?" Lochinvar asked. "Ginny and Lucy know that I have a college degree, and I thought since I'm virtually a member of your club now, that it wasn't fair to keep it a secret from the rest of you."

Lucy sighed. "Thank goodness you told them. It's agony for me to keep secrets. I don't know how Ginny can go gaily around with what she's got in her loose-leaf notebook."

Ginny glared at her. But Whiz unwittingly came to the rescue. "Oh, her English comp isn't as good as all that, even if I did help her write it. Is it supposed to be a secret, Ginny?" he teased. "What's the matter—afraid someone will swipe our deathless prose?"

Ginny poured boiling water into the top section of the coffee maker. "I don't know why Lucy thinks it's a secret," she said calmly. "I was just going to ask Lochinvar if he'd read it before I hand it in. It's about Kentucky mountaineers," she told him.

"I'd be glad to read it," he said. "I haven't been home since I was graduated from law school, but things haven't changed much since then."

Whiz whistled. "From law school? And yet you're

willing to work for us for a measly percentage of our profit! You certainly are a mystery man, Lochinvar!"

Lochinvar laughed. "I've let you Hustlers into some of the secrets of my past. How about letting me in on some of yours?"

"Why, what do you mean?" Ginny asked. "What makes you think we have secrets?"

"Well," he said, "you've got a brand new padlock on your door which is badly scratched. The screen on that window over there was recently repaired and the pane of glass was put in not long ago. The putty is much newer than the putty on the other frames." He chuckled. "I can only deduce that you kids are in the habit of locking yourselves out and leaving your keys at home. Or, that someone else has been breaking and entering." He moved down the counter to stand directly opposite Ginny. "Which deduction is correct?"

"Deduction two," she said promptly. "Tramps have been breaking in and swiping food, but nothing of any real value."

He pointed to the money in the cracker can which she had not yet finished transferring to the change compartments of the cash box. "But you don't trust your tramps, do you? Is that why you don't leave any money here overnight?"

Ginny nodded. "If they can pick the padlock they can certainly pick the lock on the petty cash box."

"Someone," he said thoughtfully, "pried the

hinges off once upon a time. Did you buy it second-hand?"

"No," Ginny told him. "A tramp pried them off, but he didn't take any of the money."

He stared at her in surprise. "Pried the hinges off but didn't take anything? That's hard for me to believe."

"I didn't say he didn't take anything," Ginny said. "I said he didn't take any money."

"What did he take?" Lochinvar asked. "Or isn't it any of my business?"

Ginny hesitated and then John said from the doorway, "Tell him, Ginny. If you talk as fast as you usually do, you'll have time before the gang gets here."

Ginny did tell Lochinvar everything then except the part about finding the second envelope, which she was sure contained five one-thousand-dollar bills. She had to whisper the last answers to his questions because boys and girls were crowding in through the doorway.

"Let's talk about this some more," he said in a low voice as he picked up his accordion. "Suppose I come back for you at closing time this afternoon and drive you home. We can toss your bike in the back of the jeep and you can give me your English composition to read then. That'll be the excuse you give the others."

Ginny nodded. "In that case I can leave when you

leave at five-thirty. Whiz will do my share of the dishwashing today if I ask him. He knows I have to turn the composition in tomorrow." Officer Bill came in then and Ginny whispered hastily, "Don't tell him anything, please. Officer Bill is an awfully good sport, but he does tease me unmercifully."

"Ary a grain o' the myxtery will I tell him," Lochinvar said. "There's time a-plenty fer that." He began to sing then, and was immediately the center of an enthralled group of boys and girls.

"The boys at the House," Officer Bill told Ginny between munches of his second Western sandwich, "are getting worked up on the subject of this being a Youth Center. I told them what a nice, well-behaved crowd you had out here yesterday. Noisy, yes, but that's the beauty of being where you are. Nobody can hear the singing and shouting, so nobody's going to complain."

That's the trouble with the place, Ginny said inwardly. *If we were nearer other houses, Chadwell wouldn't dare lurk around. Someone would hear him or dogs would bark.*

Aloud she said, "When you get ready to start a fund-raising campaign, Officer Bill, I know Dad will help with the publicity end of it."

"We're counting on that," he said, "and a big help it will be, too. In no time at all we should be able to get enough donations so we can pay you kids back for what you put into it. That is," he went on, "if you're really agreeable to having it become a community project."

"Oh, we are," Ginny said. "And although I can't speak for the others, I, myself feel that we should consider as our own donation the money we've already put into the Barn."

"No, that's too generous of you," the friendly policeman said. "You deserve to get back what you put in so you can start another project."

"We can start another project anyway," Ginny said. "We started the Swap Shop from scratch. And if Dad gives our donation some publicity, it will start the ball to rolling."

"That it would," Officer Bill agreed. "Even the most tight-fisted adult would dig down deep in his pockets when he knows how much time and labor you kids put into this place."

He left again without waiting for his change and Ginny thought, *We're lucky to have such a wonderful police force in Harristown. Officer Bill is so good to us I really shouldn't keep secrets from him.*

If Ginny hadn't been so busy at that moment, she might have impulsively run after Officer Bill and told him the whole story of the Chadwell-Henderson envelopes. But before she knew it, it was five-thirty and Lochinvar was drawling, "I'd be mighty proud, Miss Ginny, if you'd let me wagon you home."

"That's very nice of you," Ginny said and hailed Whiz. "If you'll do my share of the dishes today," she told him, "I'll do yours two days running. Loch-invar is going to drive me home and read my composition so I can make the final copy tonight."

"Go right ahead," Whiz said cheerfully. "I'll get dishpan hands but the A you'll get in English will be worth it. I owe you a little something for coaching me in math." He grinned. "There were times today when I even knew what our instructor was talking about."

"So," Lochinvar said as they climbed into his jeep, "among other things you're a math coach, Ginny Gordon."

Ginny laughed. "I only coach the twins every now and then. Whiz is really very bright although he pretends to be baffled."

"I'm baffled myself," Lochinvar said. "You talked so fast when you were telling me about Chenderson and Hadwell—"

"Chadwell and Henderson," Ginny corrected him with a giggle.

"Begin at the beginning," he begged her, "and tell me the story all over again."

Talking slowly and carefully Ginny described all the events up to the point when she had found the envelope addressed to Chadwell in the cash box. She did not mention the fact that John's piece of pine board and bottle of glue were also missing because she didn't think they were important.

"Was food missing again today?" he asked her

when she had finished.

"I couldn't really tell," Ginny said. "The shelves are so filled now I'd have to take an inventory to be sure." She hesitated, sorely tempted to share her theory of who was behind the thefts with this man who seemed so interested in the progress of the Barn. Quickly she decided not to tell him anything more. They had only known him a few days, and, in lots of ways, he was a suspicious character himself. That gun in his shoulder holster—his early morning walks —he posed as an illiterate hillbilly and yet he was a law school graduate. He, himself, was baffling.

"A penny for your thoughts," he said, parking his jeep in her driveway.

"A dollar for yours," Ginny came back with a grin. "What do you make of the mystery?"

"I'll have to think about it," he said slowly. He vaulted nimbly out of the driver's seat and took her bicycle from the back, lifting it with one hand as though it were as light as a feather.

"You certainly are strong," Ginny said, smiling. "In your spare time when you weren't going to college or law school or studying music, were you ever a prize fighter?"

He chuckled. "That's one vocation I missed in my checkered career. But I've done a lot of boxing and track."

Ginny deliberately turned her back to him as she opened her loose-leaf binder and unclipped the envelope from the pages of her English composition. Deftly she transferred it to her algebra book and turned around to face him with a smile. "Sure you don't mind reading my theme?" she asked, holding the binder out to him.

He took it with a little bow. "I'm honored. You have to have it back this evening, I imagine."

Ginny nodded. "Or early tomorrow morning. If there aren't too many corrections I can do them in the study period before English class."

"Fine," he said. "I may not get to it until late tonight, but you can count on getting it back before you leave for school tomorrow."

"I know I can count on that," Ginny said. "You're such an early riser."

He narrowed his black eyes. "And how do you know that, Ginny Gordon?"

"Because," she said, "Babs saw you before it was light on Sunday, and Lucy saw you at dawn on Monday."

He let out a long breath. "You girls certainly get around," he said ruefully. Without further comment he climbed into the driver's seat and backed out into Maple Street.

Ginny waved good-by to him and then she ran upstairs to her room. Before she did anything else she must put that envelope addressed to Mr. Chadwell in a safe place. None of her textbooks was long enough to conceal it completely. When she heard her mother calling from the kitchen, she hastily tucked the envelope beneath the paper lining of her top bureau drawer.

"I'll be right down, Mother," she called. And then she remembered too late that she had forgotten to take from her loose-leaf binder the pages on which she had written the clues which pointed the finger of suspicion to Chadwell.

Ginny sank down on her bed and covered her face with her hands. "Oh, oh," she moaned. "Lochinvar will find them when he reads my composition. I wouldn't blame him at all for reading what I wrote because we just discussed the mystery. Then he'll know that I didn't tell him about the money. And what will he think? What *will* he think?"

CHAPTER FIFTEEN

CAUSE FOR WORRY

There was only one answer to what Lochinvar would think when he read her notes, Ginny decided miserably. He would think that she hadn't told anyone about the envelope she had found in the cash box containing thousand-dollar bills, because she planned to keep the money for herself!

She began to pace up and down her room, mumbling to herself. "I've got to get my loose-leaf binder back before he starts to read my composition. After supper instead of going straight to the Reillys' to help the twins with their homework, I'll have to bike to the Inn. I'll tell Lochinvar that I left something else in my binder besides the composition. Then I'll simply tear out those sheets and leave. I can only hope that he hasn't even opened the binder since I gave it to him."

Just then the phone rang.

Ginny raced down to the library and picked up the phone.

"Hi, Ginny," John's voice said. "I was just about to sit down to supper when it suddenly occurred to me that when you left the Barn this afternoon you weren't carrying that cracker can you keep the money in."

"Oh, oh," Ginny wailed. "I left in such a hurry I forgot. It's all in the petty cash box which isn't even locked. About twenty dollars, John!"

"Never mind," he said soothingly. "I'll ride out after supper and get it."

"I'd die between now and when you got back," Ginny told him. "I'll go myself right away. It was all my fault anyway." She hung up and tore out to the kitchen. "That was John, Mother," she cried. "I did such a stupid thing. Left all our money out at the Barn and didn't even lock the cash box. Do you mind if I go and get it instead of helping you with supper?"

"Of course not," Mrs. Gordon said, smiling sympathetically. "I didn't really need you except to set the table, and there'll still be time for that when you get back. Dad phoned a while ago that he'd be late."

Ginny hurried out to the driveway where she had left her bike and in a few minutes she was pedaling furiously through the park. When she turned off the main highway into the lane she stopped in amazement. Parked in front of the Barn was Lochinvar's jeep!

"Now that is suspicious," she muttered, promptly dragging her bike into the woods. "He knows we've all gone home. I'm going to sneak up there through the evergreens and find out what he's up to."

As she trudged along the narrow path that was

thickly carpeted with pine needles she wished more
than ever that she hadn't left those pages of clues in
her loose-leaf notebook. In fact, she wished she
hadn't told Lochinvar anything. No one, apparently,
knew who he was or where he came from or what
his real reason was for being in town.

When you tried to pin him down he answered by
singing, "A Wandering Minstrel, I!" That could
mean anything. Whiz was right; it didn't make sense.
A law school graduate working for so little money!

When Ginny reached the trees across the lane
from the Barn she stopped. Lochinvar was coming
around from the back of the Barn. She could see him
plainly, but felt sure the thick branches of the blue
spruces hid her from view.

He strode purposefully to the door of the Barn,
took a tiny pair of tweezers from his pocket, and
before Ginny could blink, the bow of the padlock
was open.

She stood rooted to the spot as he disappeared
inside the Barn. If he was the man who had been
breaking into the Barn all along, nothing made any
sense any more. But it couldn't have been Lochinvar
who stole the food. One thing was sure; the Inn pro-
vided him with three good meals a day.

And it couldn't have been Lochinvar who took
the envelope addressed to Henderson from the cash
box and later replaced it with the one addressed to
Chadwell. He had no way of knowing anything

Lochinvar Was Breaking into the Barn!

about that transaction until Ginny told him.

What *was* he doing in the Barn? For a moment Ginny was tempted to hurry back to town and report what she had seen to Officer Bill. But having Lochinvar arrested for breaking and entering wouldn't solve all of the mysteries. Besides, by the time the policeman arrived on the scene, Lochinvar would surely be gone. His word was as good as hers; how could she prove that she had seen him pick the lock?

Proof, *proof*—it always came back to that! Suddenly Ginny made up her mind. Tomorrow evening she would set up a booby trap with her camera which would catch one of the three mysterious men while he was in the Barn. Somehow she would find out from John and Whiz how it could be done. Somehow she must make them believe that she wanted to take a picture of the pheasants.

And then Lochinvar came out, snapped the padlock in place and climbed into his jeep. As soon as he was out of sight, she dashed across the lane, unlocked the door and stood on the threshold staring around. Nothing looked as though it had been touched, but she hardly dared to look inside the petty cash box.

Suppose Lochinvar was a burglar? That would explain the quick deftness with which he had picked the padlock; and it would also explain why he didn't mind working for so little money. He might be staying at the Inn for the very purpose of robbing some of the rich people who lived in town. All along he might have been sneaking into their homes before dawn and taking things which hadn't yet been missed.

She thought of Mrs. Arnold's living-room, packed and jammed with valuable antiques. As far as she knew, no one ever took an inventory of the little old lady's possessions. But there was no sense in standing there, worrying. Resolutely, Ginny ducked under the counter, took the cash box off the shelf and opened it.

It was almost overflowing with quarters and dimes and nickels, and looked exactly as it had when she had left the Barn earlier. Ginny dumped the change into the cracker can and hurried out. She locked the door and ran as fast as she could down the lane to where she had dumped her bike in the woods. She had been gone a lot longer than she had expected and it was growing dark. What excuse could she give her parents?

All the way home, Ginny worried. One way to escape a scolding was, of course, to tell the truth. Then one question would lead to another, and the end of the matter would be that Ginny Gordon would have to resign as the Hustlers' treasurer.

But she couldn't deliberately lie to her parents. If they asked her why she had been gone so long, she would have to tell them the truth. Ginny sighed, and, with the heavy cracker can under her arm, wearily climbed up her front steps to the porch. In another twenty-four hours she might have solved the mystery herself. Now she wouldn't have the chance.

She stood in the hall, blinking until her eyes grew accustomed to the light, for it was really dark outside now. And then, as though in answer to a prayer, John came out of the library.

"Hi, Ginny," he said cheerfully. "Your mother called me because she got worried; you were gone so long. I've been explaining. Knowing you, I'm sure you had to count every single penny to make sure the day's receipts were intact before you left the Barn."

It was all Ginny could do to keep from letting out a long sigh of relief. Her mother and father appeared at the library door then and she said hastily, "I'm awfully sorry. I hope you didn't wait for me. Have you had your dinner?"

Mr. Gordon laughed. "No. I just got home myself."

Her mother, Ginny noticed with a sinking heart, was not even smiling. "In spite of John's explanation," she told Ginny, "I had just asked him to ride out to see what could possibly have delayed you. It gets dark so suddenly at this time of the year, and that Barn is in such an isolated spot."

"Well, I'll run along now," John said. "Homework awaits me."

After he had gone Mr. Gordon pointed to the

cracker can under Ginny's arm and asked, "What's that? Did you bring home some snacks thinking that your mother wasn't going to feed you as punishment for being late?" He grinned.

Ginny grinned back at him. "No, Dad," she explained. "It's our money. I keep out enough for change and for each day's supplies and deposit the rest in the bank during my lunch hour. It's really an awful responsibility," she added.

When they were all seated at the dining-room table, Mrs. Gordon said with a sympathetic smile, "I know it's a great responsibility being the treasurer, Ginny, and I'm sorry I got so upset when you didn't come right back. If I'd known Lucy or John were with you, I wouldn't have worried. But Lucy called right after you left."

"Oh, did she?" Ginny asked.

Mrs. Gordon nodded. "She wanted to know if you could have dinner with her tomorrow and go to the early show at the Palace."

"I'd like to very much," Ginny said. "You and Dad are going to the PTA meeting with Lucy's parents, aren't you?"

"That's right," Mrs. Gordon said. "I was sure you would accept Lucy's invitation so I invited Mr. and Mrs. Tryon to have a bite with us here before the meeting." She laughed. "Lucy said she was only going to give you a snack. She said that's all she knows how to fix. You'd better eat a good lunch in the cafeteria tomorrow."

"I will," Ginny promised. "I'm so sick of snacks
I can't look one in the eye. If Lucy produces cheeseburgers I'll faint."

Mr. Gordon chuckled. "You sound as though
you'd bit off more than you can chew, Ginny. Getting tired of the Snack Barn?"

"Well, not exactly," Ginny told him. "But it *is* a
lot more work than I thought it would be."

"I hope it isn't interfering with your school
work," he said, frowning a little. "How is your English composition going?"

And then Ginny remembered. The pages on
which she had listed her clues were still in her loose-
leaf binder!

"Why, what's the matter, Ginny?" her mother
asked. "You look so worried. Isn't your theme ready
to hand in tomorrow?"

"It is, Mother," Ginny said, "except that I asked
Lochinvar to read it."

Mr. Gordon laughed heartily. "He'll be able to
catch any glaring errors in the factual department,
but you'll be in trouble if he tries to correct your
grammar."

Ginny tried to laugh, too, but she could only
manage a weak smile. "If you don't mind," she said,
"I'd like to go to the Inn before I go to the Reillys'
this evening. Lochinvar may have read my composition by now." She glanced at her wrist watch. "It's

only seven-thirty. I can do the dishes when I get back, Mother."

Ten minutes later she was climbing the steps to the Inn's porch. When she came into the lobby she saw the manager standing beside the front desk.

"Hello, Mr. Crayne," she said. "I'm looking for Lochinvar. He hasn't started to sing yet, has he?"

"No," the manager said. "But he will in a few minutes. Now, don't you detain him, Ginny. I'll ring his room and ask him to come right down."

"Let me speak to him, please," Ginny said. "It'll save time if I talk to him before he comes down."

Mr. Crayne shrugged and handed her the desk phone. When she was connected with the White Elephant, Ginny said into the mouthpiece, "Hello, Lochinvar. This is Ginny Gordon, and I—"

"Why, hello, Ginny," he said. "I just finished reading your composition and I think it's very good. Where are you?"

"Down in the lobby," Ginny told him. *Oh, dear,* she thought, *he must have read my list of clues.*

"I'll be with you in a minute," he said and hung up.

Almost before Ginny could turn around, he was bounding down the stairs with his accordion under one arm and her loose-leaf binder under the other. Ginny couldn't help staring at him. How could he look so gay and friendly when he had just broken into their Barn?

"Like father, like daughter," he said, giving her the notebook. "You write very well, Ginny." Then as the manager moved closer to where they were standing he said in an entirely different tone of voice, "Thank you kindly fer letten me read hit." With a courteous bow, he hurried by her into the dining-room.

"Now what did he mean by that?" Ginny asked herself as she left the Inn. "Was he talking about my composition or the notes I wrote on the Henderson-Chadwell mystery?"

As soon as she got home from the Reillys' the first thing she did was to go to her room and read those pages in her notebook again. There could be no doubt of it; if Lochinvar had read her notes on the mystery he must know now that she had five thousand dollars which didn't belong to her.

If he were a burglar wouldn't he try to get the money from her? Was that why he had thanked her when he returned the notebook to her? "Thank you kindly fer letten me read hit" might have been a cryptic warning.

Ginny shivered. "Oh, dear," she moaned as she took the envelope from her drawer and clipped it to a blank page in her binder. "I wish I'd never seen any of those three mysterious men. If my camera trap doesn't work, I'll tell Dad everything on Saturday morning. I couldn't live through the week-end worrying about this money."

CHAPTER SIXTEEN

WIRE, FILM, AND A FLASH BULB

During lunch in the cafeteria on Friday, Ginny carefully maneuvered her tray so that she sat between John and Whiz.

"I think you boys are mean," she said pretending to pout. "I really do want to take a picture of those pheasants. I mean, I want to set up my camera on the tripod so that they'll take a picture of themselves."

Whiz groaned. "You know perfectly well, Ginny, that you haven't a mechanical mind. You could no more rig up a contraption that would lure a pheasant into taking its own picture than I could make a hydrogen bomb."

"I can try," Ginny told him stubbornly. "And, if I get a good shot, I'll enter it in the amateur photographers' contest. Then, when I win first prize—"

"Since when this interest in photography?" John interrupted. "The last time you took a picture of Lucy only her ear showed up on the negative."

"And since when this interest in our feathered friends?" Whiz demanded. "I remember when Granny kept chickens you were afraid to go in the coop and gather the eggs."

"That was entirely different," Ginny told him loftily. "I was a mere child, and besides, those hens on the nests were positively vicious."

"Hen pheasants on the nest," John told her, "are a lot more vicious."

"That's the point," Ginny said shrewdly. "I have no intention of going near those birds. I simply want to get a picture of them eating the crumbs in front of the Barn. Even if it doesn't win a prize I'd like it for my scrap book." She turned to Whiz. "I know you have to have a flash bulb. What else?"

"Why a flash bulb?" he asked suspiciously. "That's a sunny spot in the morning, the front of the Barn."

"And why a tripod?" John said. "The pheasants are going to be on the ground, aren't they?"

"I thought it would be dark when they came out of the woods to eat the crumbs," Ginny said. "And I thought they'd be so frightened when the flash went off that they'd fly in the air."

Whiz hooted. "Pheasants," he said, "are first cousins of chickens. Like all birds, they go to bed at dusk and don't leave their roosts until dawn. And if you expect to catch them on the wing, you'd better get high speed film."

"That's right," John said, pretending to be very serious. "The next step is to catch the pheasants and train them. One of them must peck at a certain crumb around which you have tied a piece of string. The other end of the string you will have attached to your camera so that one peck will click the shutter."

Whiz nodded soberly. "Exactly, professor. That is, always supposing that she has remembered to wind the film."

Ginny tossed her chestnut curls. "Oh, never mind, you two. The next time either of you ask a favor of me, I'll remember how co-operative you were today."

"Gleeps," Whiz yelped. "Here's where I flunk math! Does your dire threat mean no more coaching, Ginny?"

"It certainly does," she said, rising with exaggerated dignity.

"Wa-it a minute," he begged. "In that case, I'll rig it up for you, Ginny. I'll even catch a pheasant and train him so that he can take a picture of his mate and then train her to take a picture of him." He clasped his hands in mock prayer. "Anything, anything to avoid going to summer school."

Ginny ignored him. "I've lost interest in the entire project," she told John. "And please tell your friend, Whiz Reilly, that he doesn't need coaching. All he needs to do is stop clowning in class." She stalked away and carried her tray to the table where Lucy was sitting with Babs.

"You look as mad as a wet hen," Lucy began.

"Puh-leeze," Ginny interrupted. "Don't mention our feathered friends to me. I've just been forced to listen to a boring lecture on the subject by two mad scientists!"

Babs's eyes widened with surprise. "Mad scientists? Oh, Ginny, you don't suspect mad scientists of breaking into the Barn, do you?"

Ginny put her elbow on the table and rested her cheek wearily in her hand. "Honestly, Babs," she said. "Sometimes I think Whiz is right. You were born without a brain."

Lucy giggled. "The mad scientists Ginny was referring to," she told Babs, "are none other than your twin and John."

"True if ungrammatical," Ginny said, and began to eat her spaghetti.

"What was wrong with that sentence?" Lucy demanded in a hurt voice.

Ginny laughed. "I'm not sure," she admitted, "but I don't see how two can be none other."

Babs looked so confused that both girls went off into gales of laughter. "I don't understand," Babs wailed. "Why are Whiz and John mad?"

"They're not," Ginny said. "I am. Were you girls discussing our petty thief when I so rudely interrupted?"

Lucy nodded. "We were wondering if Lochinvar had any ideas on the subject. What did he say when he drove you home yesterday, Ginny?"

"He said," Ginny replied, "that he would have to think about it."

"That wasn't very helpful," Babs complained. "Anybody can think."

"Anybody but you," Lucy said with a grin. "And frankly, when I think about it I go around in circles, don't you, Ginny?"

"I go around in spirals," Ginny said. "They're much worse than circles."

They finished their lunch in silence and then Ginny said, "Well, I have to go to the bank and do some shopping. See you all later."

First she went to her locker where she had put the cracker can of money and her loose-leaf binder in the morning. The envelope was still clipped to a blank page. Ginny lived in almost constant fear that the time would come when she would open the binder and find the envelope gone.

"Thank goodness," she thought, "these lockers all have special dial locks like safes. I don't see why the boys can't fix up something like them on the Barn door."

In a few minutes she was standing in line by the cashier's window. On Fridays the lunch-hour line was even longer than usual, and by the time the cashier had finished counting the change in the cracker can, Ginny realized that she would have to do her shopping after school.

"Listen, Ginny," the cashier said when he returned the pass book to her, "I'm going to give you some change cylinders. All you have to do is fill 'em and fold 'em. They're marked plainly and hold only the amount indicated. We'll save a lot of time that way."

"Thanks," Ginny said, putting the little paper folders in the empty cracker can. "I should have asked for them before."

He smiled. "At the rate you're going, you'll soon have a large enough balance so you can open a checking account."

If he only knew, Ginny thought as she hurried back to school. *All I need to make me happy is to have five thousand dollars less than I have!*

In the study period before English Ginny hastily skimmed through her composition to see if Lochinvar had found any errors. To her relief he had made only two lightly penciled marginal notes, both of which indicated split infinitives.

Now that was nice of him, Ginny reflected. *He could have just skimmed my theme, but instead he obviously read it very carefully.* Suddenly it occurred to her that he might not have read anything else in her binder except the composition. *If he hadn't picked the lock on the Barn I would have felt sure that he is the kind of man who wouldn't read anything that didn't concern him.*

And then she was struck with another idea. Lochinvar must have felt sure that she had deliberately put her list of clues in the notebook with her composition because she *wanted* him to read those pages.

After all, just before she had given him the binder yesterday in her driveway she had asked him what he thought of the mystery. But why had he thanked her last night when he returned the binder to her?

He had no reason to be grateful for doing her the favor of checking her composition. Neither did he have any reason to be grateful for the privilege of reading what she thought was behind the mysterious behavior of the two men.

He had no reason to be grateful at all—unless he was a thief and had decided to try to get the five thousand dollars from the moment she told him about Chadwell and Henderson. That would explain why he had driven her home and asked her so many questions. It would also explain why he had gone back to the Barn shortly afterward. If he had read her notes at once he would have come to the conclusion that the envelope containing the money might well still be in the cash box which he could have noticed she had left unlocked when they left the Barn together at five-thirty. In that case, had he driven right out to the Barn, and, finding only small change in the cash box, had now come to the conclusion that Ginny had the money? Had his sharp eyes seen her when she had surreptitiously transferred the envelope from the binder to her algebra book? He must have noticed the long envelope protruding from the pages of the textbook when she said goodby to him yesterday. Was he planning to get that envelope away from her at the first opportunity?

"I'll never bring it to the Barn again," Ginny decided. "This afternoon I'll put my binder in the bottom drawer of Dad's desk under a pile of old receipted bills."

But in spite of everything, Ginny couldn't quite make herself believe that the friendly singer was a dishonest person. He had gone out of his way to be kind to all of them.

Ginny had always intuitively disliked every dishonest person she had ever known. And she had instinctively liked—even admired, Lochinvar the moment she saw him. His shrewd eyes apparently missed nothing, but they were the clear, wide eyes of an intelligent, honest citizen.

"Oh, dear," she sighed. "I'm thinking in spirals again and that's a waste of time."

"If I keep on thinking about the mystery," she told Lucy later in front of the school, "I'll spiral right off into the stratosphere."

"Don't do that," Lucy begged with a giggle. "Then they'll make me treasurer, and that would be the final blow!"

Ginny drew herself up into a very regal pose and tapped Lucy lightly on the forehead with her ruler. "I hereby dub thee treasurer for the next hour. I'm going to be late reporting for duty at the Barn today."

"Why?" Lucy demanded suspiciously.

Ginny straddled her bike. "I'll explain while we ride to Main Street." As they pedaled along, side by side, she went on, "I've got some shopping to do."

"I know," Lucy said. "You told me this morning. We need bread and cheese and hamburger and olives."

"No," Ginny said firmly. "You'll buy those."

"With what?" Lucy asked. "As usual, this being allowance day, I haven't a cent."

"All of the Barn's petty cash," Ginny told her, "is in a wool sock in my top bureau drawer, and so is the key to the cash box. You don't need the key to the padlock because the boys always get there first."

"I know," Lucy said petulantly. "It seems to me an unfair division of labor. We have to buy the food and fix it every single day, day after day. All Whiz and Babs do is eat it and serve it, with accent on *eat*."

"Don't forget," Ginny said, "John serves all the cold drinks and washes and dries every single glass every single day, day after day, and is responsible for the ice department. Whiz and Babs never have a chance to sit down until after we stop serving food, and every other day they wash and dry the dishes."

Lucy blushed with embarrassment. "Oh, I know, Ginny. And you work harder than all of us. It must be an awful chore to count the money and take it to the bank every day."

"I'm glad you feel that way about it," Ginny said, smiling. "Then you won't mind pinch-hitting for me just this once?"

"Of course not," Lucy said. "But I am curious to know what kind of shopping *you* are going to do. You don't need any clothes, Ginny. Your mother bought you every single thing any girl could ever want before school opened last month."

"If you promise not to tell," Ginny said with a mischievous laugh as they stopped for the light on the corner of Main and Maple Streets, "Hilliker's is having a white sale. Like mother, like daughter, remember?"

And although Lucy plied her with questions until they separated on the opposite corner, Ginny wouldn't say another word. She biked down Main Street to the department store and went straight to the sports department. From the clerk at the counter where photographers' supplies were displayed, she bought a flash bulb and a roll of high-speed film. At another counter she bought a yard of fine wire. After carefully putting these purchases in the cracker can which she had left outside in her bike basket, she rode home for her camera.

Ginny was hastily putting the speed film in her camera when Lila appeared at the door of the library.

"Lucy," the maid said hoarsely, "was rummaging around in your room a little while ago, Ginny. She went off with a sock that bulged at the toe as though your mother's darning egg was in it. It didn't seem right to me, but what could I do?"

Ginny laughed. "I'm glad your cold is better, Lila. We certainly did miss you."

"I'm sure you did," Lila said with a grin. "What was in the toe of the sock?"

"Money," Ginny told her. "The Barn's petty cash."

Lila placed her tiny hands on her slim hips. "Then why was it up in your room? Petty cash belongs in a petty cash box. At least it did when I went to school not so long ago."

Ginny closed her box camera. "You're absolutely right, Lila," she said. "But we've been having trouble with tramps. Don't tell Mother and Dad. I'm going to tell them all about it myself tomorrow."

Ginny knew she could trust Lila who was only a few years older than she, and had come to work for the Gordons straight from high school.

Lila smiled, flashing her white even teeth. "You're up to another mystery," she said shrewdly, "and that camera has something to do with it."

"It has," Ginny admitted. "But it's a secret."

Lila sniffed. "It may be a secret to some people, but it's as plain as the nose on your face to me."

Ginny sighed. "Okay, okay, Lila. I'm going to try to make our tramp take a picture of himself tonight. I'll have the film developed tomorrow and give the print to Officer Bill."

Lila tucked her hands in the pockets of her dainty

organdy apron. "And how," she asked, "are you going to make said tramp photograph himself?"

"I'm not sure my trap will work," Ginny admitted, "but what I'm going to do is this. The tramp is forever swiping things from our refrigerator. So I'm going to take out the forty-watt bulb and put a flash bulb in its place. Then I'm going to attach a fine piece of wire to the handle of the refrigerator and hook the other end of it around the finger release on my camera. I'll set the camera on my tripod beside the refrigerator door and focus it so that when the tramp opens the door the bulb will flash and the shutter will click, and tomorrow morning I'll have a snapshot of his face."

"Very clever," Lila said with growing interest, "except for one thing. If the camera is on the tripod it may topple to the floor when he pulls the wire taut. If I were you, I'd anchor it somehow to the counter which ends right there by the refrigerator. And it's just about the right height, because Mr. Tramp will be stooping slightly when he snoops."

Ginny giggled. "You're very smart, Lila. Why are you so good to me?"

"I'll tell you why," Lila said rather grimly. "Because this sounds like one mystery you're going to try to solve without being at the scene of the crime." She shook her head solemnly. "The last two traps you set almost trapped you."

"I know, I know," Ginny said, leading the w

out to the porch. "But this time there is no danger of that. So keep it all under your cute little charlotte russe cap, won't you, Lila?"

Lila gave her a conspiratorial nod as Ginny biked off, so she felt sure that her secret was safe with the pretty little maid.

When she arrived at the foot of the lane, Ginny hid her camera and her purchases in the woods, then she biked on to the Barn.

"There's no danger at all," she thought exultantly, "and Lila, who is very smart, thinks it may work. By this time tomorrow we should know who has been stealing our food. And unless I'm all wrong in my reasoning, that *who* just has to be Mr. Blackmailing Chadwell!"

CHAPTER SEVENTEEN

AN UNWELCOME CALLER

The early show at the Palace Theater started at seven, so by six o'clock on Friday afternoon, every young customer had left the Barn.

"How do you like that?" Whiz demanded from the doorway. "I thought the crowd would stay late on account of no homework tonight. Is the Palace going to cut in on our business?"

"On the contrary," said Ginny who had just finished counting the day's receipts. "We stop serving food at five-thirty anyway. And, because a lot of folks have supper after the show instead of an early dinner on Fridays, we sold twice as many snacks as usual. In fact," she finished excitedly, "we took in twenty-nine dollars and fifty-five cents!"

Whiz whistled. "I'm glad I don't have to wash all those plates and cups and saucers. They're yours, Ginny, all yours."

He left and Babs wailed, "Oh, please, can't I go, too? I know it's my turn, Lucy, but we'll be late to the show and then we can't get a seat down near the front."

Lucy glared at her. "Has it ever occurred to you that other people like good seats, too?"

"All of you go," Ginny said quickly. "I don't care a thing about seeing that movie."

"Why, Ginny," Babs cried in a shocked tone of voice. "It's a Western!"

"I know," Ginny said placidly as she dumped soapsuds into the sink. "But lately I haven't been able to tell the difference between the outlaws and the posse. Go on, Babs, and catch up with Whiz."

Babs darted out, and John, from the opposite sink, laughed. "Old age is catching up with you, Ginny. You used to love Westerns."

"She still does," Lucy cried exasperatedly. "I keep telling you she's too generous for her own good." She came back of the counter to join Ginny at the sink. "I'm not going to leave you with that stack of dishes even if it is your own fault."

"Scram," Ginny said, elbowing her away. "I'll get there in time for the animated cartoon which I wouldn't miss for anything."

"Now, she's in her second childhood," John said, putting away the last sparkling glass. "Although I must admit I'm a cartoon fan myself." He ducked under the counter and crossed over to the girls. "Run along, Lucy," he said. "I'll help Ginny and we'll both get there before seven. I'm far-sighted so I have to sit far back anyway in order to tell the difference between the sheriff and the crook."

Ginny giggled although inwardly she was seething. Why couldn't they both go home and leave her alone so she could set up her camera trap? "Don't be so big-hearted, John," she said. "You must have washed and dried and put away a million glasses today. And I got off early yesterday."

"I have spoken," John said firmly, pointing over his shoulder with his thumb. "Go, Lucy. It is my wish."

"We-ell," Lucy said weakly. "If you really don't mind, John." She came out from behind the counter and started for the door. "You don't mind either, Ginny?"

"I, too, have spoken," Ginny said wearily. "I'll meet you by the ticket booth after the show, Lucy. And you be sure that you're not going to give me cheeseburgers for supper."

"Oh, no," Lucy cried. "I wouldn't think of it. I'm going to make a mushroom omelet. It tells how on the mushroom can. Why don't you have supper with us, John? Your parents will be at the PTA meeting, too, won't they?"

"I accept," John said with a little bow, and added to Ginny in an undertone, "although I don't really care for leather-hash which is what her omelet will be."

"It won't be anything of the kind," Ginny said rather crossly. "Lucy is very good at following directions, which you aren't. Please go; you make me nervous standing there wringing that dish towel when I haven't even rinsed the plates yet."

John swung himself up on the counter. "Don't hurry on account of me, Ginny," he said cheerfully. "So we took in almost thirty dollars?"

Ginny nodded. "Almost everybody ordered soup and salad and dessert besides sandwiches and drinks. Their parents gave them the money so they could go straight to the movies from here." *I wish you'd go straight to the movies from here, right now,* she added silently.

"Say, that's something," John said enthusiastically. "We'll make as much on Fridays as we do on Saturdays and Sundays."

"That's right," Ginny said. "We're all out of everything I ordered ahead of time for lunches and brunches. I'll have to go to the store the first thing tomorrow." *Well, not the very first thing,* she reflected with a smile. *The first thing I'll do is come out here and see what I caught in my little trap. If John ever leaves me alone long enough so I can set it.*

In the end, Ginny had to ride all the way in to the park with John. When they reached the short cut she said, "You go ahead and save me a seat in the back row, John. I don't want to hold this heavy old cracker can on my lap all evening. I'll cut through the park and leave it off at home with Lila."

John rode off toward Main Street without further delay, and as soon as he turned the corner by Shoemaker's, Ginny set off in the opposite direction. "I *will* stop off and leave the money with Lila," she promised herself, "but first I'll set up my camera."

By the time she passed Lucy's house it was growing dark, so she stopped in the garage to borrow the flashlight she knew Mr. Tryon always kept on a shelf. Then she biked out to the lane. Once she left the main highway and entered the woods it was so dark she had to use the flashlight to find her equipment. Then when she came out of the woods she saw to her surprise that a light was burning in the Barn.

"I'm absolutely positive John and I turned them all off," she said to herself and decided to walk to the Barn instead of riding. "I'll bet I know who's in there. Lochinvar! It's only just seven o'clock. He knew we were going to close early because of the show."

As she hurried along the lane that was strewn with autumn leaves, Ginny couldn't help smiling. "I'm not the least bit afraid of him, even if he does carry a gun. He's nice, in spite of the fact that he's an expert lock-picker. And tonight I'm going to find out why he picks our lock. I'll go right in through the door without making a sound and then I'll suddenly yell, 'Aha, my good singing lawyer, I've caught you in the act. What seems to be our fatal fascination?'"

By that time Ginny had reached the closed door of the Barn. It was unlocked and she opened it stealthily. Then she did not utter one word she had planned. Instead she stood there, staring, her lips parted with surprise.

For sitting on the stool behind the counter, his cheeks bulging with the food he was cramming into his mouth, was a fat little man in a rumpled suit.

Henderson!

He caught sight of her at the same moment that she saw him, and seemed equally surprised. Ginny broke the silence. Suddenly the sight of the fat little man whom she had interrupted while he was eating greedily, struck her as being hilariously funny. She was no more afraid of him than she was of Lochinvar and she moved over to the counter, laughing.

"Henderson!" She chuckled. "Who would have thought it? I expected your friend Chadwell sometime this evening, but not you."

He reached across the counter and grabbed her arm so roughly that her camera, equipment and the cracker can crashed to the floor.

"Scream," he rasped, "and I'll twist your arm. *Hard!*"

Taken completely off guard, Ginny did nothing but stare at him.

"So Chadwell's coming tonight?" his hoarse voice continued. "Is he bringing the books?"

Ginny tried to pull away from him but he only held her arm in a tighter grasp. "I don't know what you're talking about," she stormed. "And you'd better let me go."

He shook her roughly. "You said you expected

him this evening. Did you give him the envelope I left in your cash box?"

"I certainly did not," Ginny said coolly. "For the simple reason that I've never seen him since the day he gave me the envelope which you *stole* from our cash box." Little by little she was growing frightened but she had no intention of letting this man know it.

"Then why did you say you expected him?" Henderson demanded suspiciously.

Ginny sighed. "Must you dig your dirty fingers into my arm while you ask me silly questions?" He loosened his grip slightly and she went on, "I said that because I thought it was Chadwell who has been stealing our food every night. I should have known it was you. You've got that hoarse voice because you've been hiding in the woods and it gets cold at night."

While she talked, Ginny was thinking wildly. *If I can only make him let go of my arm. I could be out of the door before he could duck under the counter.*

"Stop gabbing," he interrupted. "Gimme that envelope. I'm going to blow tonight, and I'm not going south on the hog. I'm going well-heeled. *Hand over that envelope.*"

Ginny tossed her head. "If you'd only talk English we'd get along better."

"You understand me," he said harshly. "I need plenty of money and there's five grand in that envelope. Gimme!"

"Hand Over the Envelope!" He Snarled

"How can I open the cash box," Ginny demanded, hoping that he would release her, "with you clinging to my arm?"

But a wicked smile creased his fat face. "Don't gimme none of that," he jeered. "I already looked in the cash box. Where is it?"

"At home," Ginny told him, forcing herself to smile back at him. "In the bottom drawer of my father's desk in the library. In case you're planning to go and get it, it's clipped to a blank page in my loose-leaf binder." She shrugged airily. "Better still, why don't I go and get it for you?"

His thick lips curled. "You'd go all right, but you'd come back with that big harness bull who hangs around here every afternoon. If it hadn't been for him—"

"If you're referring to Officer Bill," Ginny interrupted, "I advise you not to call him silly, senseless names. He's a very good friend of mine and I won't answer any more of your questions unless you speak of him with respect."

"You'll answer my questions all right," he sneered. "Unless you want a broken arm." At that he dragged her down to the end of the counter and joined her on the other side. "What's in that can?" he asked, pointing. "Jingled like it was full of money when you dropped it."

"I didn't drop it," Ginny returned stanchly although her knees were shaking. "You knocked it out from under my arm."

"So it *is* full of money?" he asked with an evil leer. "I'll take it along with me and as much food as I can carry."

I can't let him take our money, Ginny thought miserably. *But how can I stop him?* She swallowed hard and said, "You'd better not waste time packing up food. You'd better leave right away. Officer Bill will be here any minute."

She knew perfectly well that the big policeman was probably home for he didn't go on duty until eight. But she had frightened this man once before with the magic phrase, *Officer Bill.* It might work again.

But it didn't. Henderson grinned. "Don't gimme that. The bull who came out here last night didn't show up until nine. I know coppers. They work like clocks. He'll show up at nine again tonight. By that time, I'll have blowed."

Ginny stared at him. "A policeman was out here last night? I don't believe it. He would have caught you stuffing yourself with our food."

"Not me," he said. "I get hungry early. I watch from the trees on the other side of the road until the last of you punks leave. Then I go in have a feast."

"You didn't do that last night," Ginny said. "I came back after the others had left, so I know."

He frowned at her. "I was late having my snack last night," he said, "because just as I was about to come out of the woods, I seen a jeep coming up from the main road. I ducked back to my hiding place. And I stayed there for about an hour. That's how I happened to see the copper. I had just left here when I seen him coming up on his motorcycle."

Ginny did not know whether to believe Henderson or not. She had never heard of motorcycle policemen patrolling the lane, and doubted if they ever did.

"Policemen," she said with forced airiness, "don't work like clocks, in case you're interested. They work according to a well-organized plan. You should have blowed or blown or whatever you call it last night as soon as you saw that officer. Why didn't you?"

"Because," he said, glancing around the room, "I kep' thinkin' Chad would give you the books. But my week's up tonight. He'll sing to the G-men, that knocker, all because you didn't give him the five grand." He glared at her. "Got any rope?"

"No, I haven't," Ginny said tartly. "And even if I had an inch of basting thread I wouldn't give it to you. If you think you're going to carry off a big bundle of our food, you're crazy. You won't get far if G-men are after you. Not after I—"

"I may not get far," he snarled, "but you won't squawk. And with a break, I might even—" He stopped, staring down at his feet.

The little roll of wire she had bought for her

camera trap had bounced down to the end of the counter when Henderson had knocked it from her hand. He stooped now and picked it up.

"This'll serve nicely for tying your hands behind your back," he said with a cruel chuckle. "If you try to wriggle loose, it'll cut your wrists to the bone. And one of them dish towels will do as a gag."

"You don't have to gag me," she told him shrewdly. "I'm not going to get hoarse from screaming for help after you leave. No one could hear me."

He unwound the wire, using his teeth and one hand. "I know what you're thinking," he said coldly. "You're thinking that you'll be here when the copper shows up. But you won't. You'll be in my hideout, and they'll never find you there. Not without bloodhounds."

Ginny shuddered. He forced her to hold her hands behind her back and wound the wire around her wrists. There was no point in struggling. She knew that she was up against a desperate criminal. Anyone who would bind and gag a young girl and leave her someplace where she might not be found until it was too late, was desperate. In order to keep her teeth from chattering she asked in what she hoped was a nonchalant voice:

"Just where *is* your hide-out? I'd like to know a little about where I'm going."

"You'll like it," he jeered. "You'll fit in it more comfy than I did. It's a regular little nest. A dried-up pool in the thickest part of the woods, filled with leaves. I stumbled into it, that's how I found it."

"Pooh," Ginny said with relief. "They'll find me there in no time."

"No, they won't," he said, pushing her into a chair. "They didn't find me, although once your harness bull pal walked right over my head."

Now he was stuffing his pockets with all the canned goods he could cram into them. "I think you're crazy," Ginny said, and really meant it. "How could he have walked over your head?"

"Because," he explained, chuckling, "your little nest has a cover. A nice piece of pine board thickly covered with leaves and pine needles. It looks just like nature made it, little girl."

So that was the explanation of the missing board and John's glue! "Whenever I hear anyone coming," Henderson went on, inspecting the inside of the refrigerator, "I hop into my little nest and cover myself up. I've been sleeping there nights, too. You'll like it. Cozy, but damp and cold." He grinned at her. "Don't worry. I'll fix you so you won't be able to make a sound or kick the cover off." He started away from the refrigerator toward the cracker can.

Ginny got up. He turned swiftly. "Sit down," he rasped, "or I'll wire you to that chair."

"Oh, no, you won't," a voice said from the darkness of the doorway. "You'll have to wire me to a chair first!" It was John, his fists clenched, moving swiftly and lightly toward the fat little man.

Then Ginny screamed. "Watch out, John! I'm sure he has a gun. He's—he's a dangerous—"

Henderson grabbed up the heavy cracker can and hurled it at John. John ducked and the can hurtled through the window they had repaired only a few days ago. It shattered the new pane of glass and ripped away the screen.

Henderson lowered his head, his big fists clenched in front of him, and Ginny knew that tall, slender John, strong as he was, could not hope to block the path of the heavy, desperate fugitive.

Before Henderson knocks John out, she thought wildly, *he'll hurt him. I can't stand it.* And she crept silently up behind the fat little man. When she stuck out her foot, he sprawled headlong to the floor, falling across the package Ginny had dropped beside the counter earlier, smashing the flashbulb to bits.

Above the sound of the small explosion, came a cold, crisp voice from the darkness of the doorway. "Stay where you are, Henderson. I've got you covered!"

Ginny could not believe her eyes. In through the door strode Lochinvar, a revolver in one hand, gleaming handcuffs dangling from the other. "This is your FBI," he said sardonically to Henderson as he manacled the fat man's hands together. "Special Agent Lockwood!" There was a chuckle in his voice as he added quietly, "Thanks again, Ginny."

CHAPTER EIGHTEEN

THE END AND A BEGINNING

The Hustlers met at the Barn right after breakfast on Saturday morning, and each one of them carried an early edition of the *News*. Ginny was the last to arrive.

Lucy met her at the door and held the headlines under her nose. "There's so much I still don't understand," she wailed. "Anyone could tell you helped your father write this thing. It reads just the way you talk. Completely over my head."

Ginny laughed. "I didn't write it. I simply dished out facts. Fast." She frowned. "I don't suppose any of you remembered that we're still in business. I had to order tons of food and practically get on my knees to Mr. Jones in order to make sure he'd deliver it before the lunch crowd arrives."

"I'll bet you did," John said, smiling. "A heroine on her knees! Why, you're on a pedestal, Ginny."

"I am not," Ginny said, hurrying behind the counter to don her apron. "But you *are* a hero, John. The way you went for that Henderson even after I warned you that he was probably armed!"

"But he wasn't," John said, "although from the way his pockets bulged he might have been carrying a sub-machine gun."

"Lochinvar," Ginny said, scrubbing her hands, "I mean, Special Agent Lockwood—"

"Oh, let's call him Lochinvar," Lucy interrupted. "Everything is so confusing anyway. Are all FBI agents such supermen?"

"They are," John said. "Some of them have as many as four degrees from colleges and universities and are skilled in all sorts of sports, trades, and professions."

"I finally got Dad to explain to me why the FBI came into it," Babs said proudly. "Income tax evasion is a federal offense and G-men are our government's private detectives."

"That's good enough for you," Whiz said. "Begin at the beginning, Ginny, and tell us ALL."

"I will," Ginny said, "if you'll all help make sandwiches, soup, and salad. We'll have a bigger crowd today than we did last Saturday." She giggled. "You should have heard what Lochinvar said last night when I tried to make him accept twenty-five per cent of our profits before he left with Henderson."

"What did he say?" Whiz asked curiously.

"He said that if he accepted any money for entertaining here, he'd have to report us to Officer Bill for operating without a cabaret license." Ginny laughed. "He didn't accept any money from the Inn either for the same reason. Mr. Crayne applied for a cabaret license, but hasn't received one yet."

While they worked Ginny told the story as she had heard it from Lockwood the night before. For a long time police officers in several different cities on the East Coast had suspected Henderson of committing robberies. But they could not obtain enough evidence to prove their suspicions, so they called on the FBI for help.

Lockwood was put on the case to get evidence of income tax evasion. "Henderson," Ginny said, "was tipped off when he was in Florida and immediately started north for his Westchester hide-out in the next town. He had a lot of money in five different savings accounts under five different names in various cities, but he didn't dare go near those banks for fear the FBI had sent his description to them.

"Chadwell, a notorious underworld blackmailer, had also heard through the grapevine that G-men were on Henderson's trail. When Henderson arrived at his hide-out, Chadwell was there waiting for him with a gun. He made Henderson give him his own gun and the five pass books and told him that if he wanted them back he would have to produce five one-thousand-dollar bills in a week. If he didn't produce the money at the end of that time, Chadwell would send the books to the FBI headquarters with a note saying that the different names were Henderson's aliases."

"And," Whiz put in, "the way the FBI works, in a few hours, they would have sent Henderson's de-

scription to those banks and had all the evidence
they needed to convict Henderson when his case
came up for trial."

"That's right," Ginny said. "Henderson was naturally terrified. He sold everything he had except
the clothes he was wearing in order to raise the
extortion money. He didn't dare meet Chadwell in
a public place for fear of being picked up by a
G-man, but neither did he dare meet him in an
isolated spot. Chadwell might well have held him up
again, taken the money away from him and kept the
pass books for further blackmailing. That's how I
came into the picture."

"I'm beginning to get it," Lucy said. "They read
about the Snack Barn opening in the local paper and
that you were our treasurer. They decided to make
you their go-between?"

Ginny nodded. "They knew what I looked like
from the group picture of us that Dad published
with the write-up, and I played right into their
hands by staying on after the rest of you left on the
opening day. They didn't read the notice very carefully and took it for granted that we served dinners,
too. Chadwell was to give me the pass books in a
sealed envelope at eight-thirty, and Henderson was
to give me the money for them at nine. Then Chadwell was to come back for the money at brunchtime
on Sunday."

"I don't see why Chadwell agreed to those terms,"

Whiz said. "Henderson might have got the pass books from you without giving you the money. He tried to, heaven knows, and in the end he did steal the envelope in which he thought they were."

Ginny smiled. "Chadwell couldn't lose, because he planned to doublecross his victim from the beginning. He counted on the fact that Henderson was terrified of G-men. He was sure that he would give me the money, grab the envelope and go back to his hide-out as quickly as possible. Too late he would find out that he had been tricked, and then the blackmailing would have started all over again."

"Why didn't Henderson show up at nine?" Babs asked.

"Because," Ginny explained, "on the way over here from his hide-out in the next town, he kept to the woods. Before he came out, he naturally peered around to make sure the coast was clear. And whom should he see coming along the highway at the foot of the lane but Officer Bill."

"Officer Bill!" Lucy gasped. "He didn't stay at the opening party long and never came back."

"He didn't come back to the Barn," Ginny told her, "but he came back to search the woods again. As a matter of fact, he only came to the Barn because he was covering every inch of Harristown on the trail of Chadwell."

"Chadwell?" Babs moaned. "I thought they were after Henderson."

"This is what happened," Ginny said, grinning. "Lochinvar, who had followed Henderson's trail to this part of Westchester, arrived at the Inn for lunch last Saturday and decided to make it his headquarters. Unfortunately for Chadwell, he arrived there while Lochinvar was talking to Mr. Crayne. Chadwell, of course, didn't know who Lochinvar was, but Lochinvar knew that Chadwell was a notorious underworld blackmailer. Suspecting that he might be blackmailing Henderson, Lochinvar secretly got in touch with Officer Bill and told him to pick up Chadwell on a vagrancy charge and hold him for questioning."

"Well," Lucy said, tossing salad in a big wooden bowl, "I'm glad somebody got arrested for vagrancy."

Whiz hooted. "No wonder Officer Bill almost died laughing when you told him to pick up Special Agent Lockwood on a vagrancy charge. And no wonder he almost lost his temper last Sunday when Mike kept insisting that Kentucky mountaineers were skinny, half-starved people. A lot of talk like that might have ruined Lockwood's disguise."

"Even Mr. Crayne," Ginny said, "had to be kept in the dark. Only the police knew who Lochinvar really was. As soon as Officer Bill got his secret orders, he set off to find Chadwell. And he finally caught up with him at the foot of the lane right after Chadwell gave me the envelope for Henderson."

John chuckled. "Henderson caught a glimpse of

Officer Bill just before that and ducked back into the woods so he didn't see the arrest. It was then that he stumbled into the dried-up pool and stayed there shaking with fright until late that night. He swiped the piece of pine board for a cover and Sunday night when he broke in, swiped the glue so he could camouflage it with leaves and pine needles."

"Sunday morning," Ginny said, "he finally got up enough courage to come to the Barn and get the pass books from me and almost walked into Officer Bill's arms when he and Mike appeared for Sunday brunch." She giggled. "That did something to the coward's nerves. No wonder he was so furtive and jittery when he finally did appear and asked me for the envelope. If he had known that Chadwell had been arrested the day before he would probably have died of fright. Because, of course, when Chadwell couldn't prove to the police how he was making a living, he was booked on a vagrancy charge and searched. When they found those pass books, Chadwell immediately confessed that they belonged to Henderson and that he had been using them for extortion."

"The arrest," John added, "was all very hush-hush, of course. Everything, like Lochinvar's identity, had to be kept a strict secret. He communicated with the police sometimes when he went for early morning walks. And that's why he never locked his room or had maid service. Messages in code were often left there, mainly between the pleats of his accordion."

Babs covered her face with both hands. "I suppose," she mumbled sheepishly, "that's why he left it in the hall by the front door Sunday when I—I—"

"That's right," Ginny said. "In the accordion was a teletyped code message from Washington stating that, after checking with the five bank officials, Henderson's description fit that of the owner of the pass books. Lochinvar had met Officer Bill early Sunday morning to arrange that the report would be put in the accordion as soon as it arrived. Lochinvar purposely left it on the hall table when he saw one of our detectives coming up the front steps of the Inn just before you did, Babs. Then he carefully left the coast clear by going into the dining-room and singing. The police detective put the report in the accordion and left. A few minutes later Lochinvar came back for the accordion and found it gone. You can imagine how baffled he was."

"And because of you," Whiz yelled at Babs, "he didn't receive the report until late Sunday afternoon when John and Ginny hinted that it might be in his room." He turned to Ginny. "So I suppose it wasn't until Monday that every police officer in this whole area was alerted to watch out for Henderson?"

Ginny nodded. "Now, don't cry, Babs. We all made it just as hard for Lochinvar as we could. If I hadn't insisted upon keeping all the mysterious events a secret, the police would have captured Henderson long ago." She blushed. "I suspected Chadwell, but of course, the minute Lochinvar read my list of clues, which he naturally thought I had left in my notebook for him to read, he knew that it was Henderson who had been stealing our food."

"What I don't understand," Lucy said, "is why Henderson broke in the first night and picked the lock after that."

"The first night," Ginny explained, "Henderson didn't have to be cagey because he planned to get the pass books from our cash box and leave the country. When he opened the envelope in his hide-out and discovered that he had been tricked, he at first thought that *we* had substituted the blank envelopes for the pass books. He didn't dare break in through a window again for fear of arousing the attention of the police, so he picked the lock and kept searching every night for the pass books, and, incidentally, took food which he didn't think we'd miss. Finally he came to the conclusion that Chadwell had tried to doublecross him. Terrified for fear Chadwell might turn the pass books over to the FBI, he left the five thousand dollars in our cash box early Wednesday morning. I was his only go-between, you see, and he hoped that when I gave Chadwell the money, Chadwell might give me the pass books. He had no way of knowing that Chadwell had been arrested."

"Then I was right," Lucy said with a little shiver. "He heard someone coming up the lane early Wednesday morning and left in such a hurry he didn't snap the bow of the padlock. That someone was you, Ginny."

"What baffles me," Whiz said, "is why Lochinvar didn't have the woods across the road combed the minute he read your list of clues."

"For several reasons," Ginny told him. "The woods had already been combed several times, and I didn't list among my clues the fact that John's piece of board and glue were missing. If I had, Lochinvar would have known that they had been used to camouflage Henderson's hide-out, but even then I don't think he would have acted differently."

"Why not?" Lucy demanded.

"I can answer that one," Whiz said. "The FBI is dead against gunplay unless it can't be helped. They wait patiently for hours and sometimes days to capture a criminal rather than shooting it out with him and risk killing or wounding innocent bystanders."

"That's right," Ginny said soberly. "And Lochinvar was sure Henderson could be captured without any trouble at all the very next time he sneaked into our Barn. Right after I discussed the mystery with him on Thursday, Lochinvar went to the Barn himself and looked all around the outside and inside for clues, although he was pretty sure that our tramp was Henderson. Then he went back to the Inn, and as soon as he possibly could, without arousing the suspicion of Mr. Crayne, sent word to police headquarters, asking that an officer be assigned to the duty of guarding the Barn all that night. Unfortunately, the officer missed Henderson by literally seconds. So Lochinvar decided that he'd guard the Barn himself the next night, last night, even if it meant a scene with Mr. Crayne during which he would have to reveal his real identity."

"And, boy, was it ever a scene!" John interrupted with a grin. "According to Lochinvar, when he told Mr. Crayne that he wasn't going to appear on Friday night, one of the Inn's big nights, the manager practically had a convulsion. Even when Lochinvar produced his badge and credentials, Mr. Crayne was too upset to believe him for quite a while."

Ginny laughed. "Lochinvar admits that for once he played his part too well. But he had to calm Mr. Crayne's nerves and swear him to secrecy before he left the Inn. He wasn't absolutely sure, you see, that he would capture Henderson last night, and until the criminal was actually handcuffed, Lochinvar's identity had to be kept a secret. Anyway," she went on, "that's why he was late arriving at the Barn."

John took up the story then. "Like me, when he turned into the lane—"

"By the way," Ginny interrupted, "how did you happen to show up when you did? I thought you were at the movies."

"I was," John said with a grin, "waiting for you. And while I waited, and waited, I got to thinking about you and your pheasants. Then, all of a sudden, it dawned on me that you were probably up to your old trick of setting a trap for a crook, not birds. So I came back. When I turned into the lane and saw lights in the Barn, I sneaked up to the door to see what you were up to. What I saw almost threw me. Whew!" He smoothed his dark hair back from his forehead and said to the others, "Ginny with her hands behind her back and that fat little man snarling at her!"

"It was a nasty moment," Ginny admitted. "And if you think you were surprised by what you saw, imagine how Lochinvar felt. When he arrived at the foot of the lane and saw lights in here, he parked his jeep and came up quietly to the door, feeling sure that he would catch Henderson rifling our refrigerator. What *he* saw almost threw *him*. He didn't dare use his gun because he had no way of knowing that Henderson wasn't armed and wouldn't try to shoot his way out. In that case, John and I would have got hurt."

"It was a nasty moment for Lochinvar, too," John said, grinning, "until Ginny tripped up Henderson and sent him sprawling."

"I don't know how you did it, Ginny," Lucy gasped. "With your hands tied behind your back and your knees shaking, and you thought Henderson had a gun."

"Ginny's a real heroine all right," Babs said seriously. "She helped a G-man capture a criminal! The only thing I don't understand now is why Lochinvar was so careful to keep his secret from Mr. Crayne, and yet he practically told us that he was a G-man."

"He didn't do anything of the kind," Whiz retorted. "Can't you see? From the first day he sang out here he realized that something mysterious was going on. When we didn't confide in him, he decided that we might if he broke down and told us he knew a little something about the law of the land."

"But Ginny and Lucy," Babs protested. "He told them that he was a college graduate right off."

"He did that," Ginny told Babs, "because you and Lucy had worn him down with your silly tricks. He thought you might stop if you knew he wasn't an illiterate hillbilly."

Lucy glared at Babs. "He thought then that I was guilty of all the crimes just because he'd caught me playing ghost. I suppose he still thinks it was I who let the air out of the jeep's tires."

"You know," Ginny said thoughtfully, "that was the only fib I ever heard of Officer Bill telling. Lochinvar never told him that he let the air out of people's tires when he was a kid. Officer Bill just said that because he felt so sorry for Babs. He felt sorry for all of us because he couldn't tell us who Lochinvar really was."

"Ginny's a Real Heroine!"

"He's some guy, Officer Bill," Whiz said.

"He's our best friend," Ginny went on. "I suppose you all know what happened at the PTA meeting last night?"

"I don't," Lucy said. "What did happen?"

"Don't you kids read the paper?" Ginny asked with an impish grin. "It's right there on the front page. They unanimously voted that as of Monday the Snack Barn is a community project. Officer Bill promoted the idea. And it's to be run exactly the way we've been running it, only on a grander scale. Our parents and teachers are going to take turns chaperoning the parties and supervising sports events. And the best thing of all is that every boy and girl who goes to High will take turns working here. Sometimes as treasurer, sometimes serving or cooking. And talented ones will entertain."

"It's simply wonderful," Lucy cried enthusiastically. "It means we won't lose the Barn, we'll simply share it."

"That's right," John said. "And we need help. We really did bite off more than we could chew this time."

"The oil burner," Ginny said, "is to be installed over the week-end. And every cent we have spent will be deposited to our account in the bank on Monday."

There was a long silence and then Whiz said, "I never really thought of that account as ours. I thought of it as the Snack Barn's."

"Me, too," Lucy and Babs cried together.

John nodded. "That's the way Ginny and I feel about it. So why don't we just leave it in the bank?"

"Suits me," Whiz said. "Some day it might mean a college education for some boy or girl not as lucky as we are. Someone like Joe Dakor, for instance, who had to quit college when his father died so he could support his mother."

"Oh, Whiz," Ginny cried excitedly. "I hoped you'd say that. The five hundred dollars we got for the Swap Shop has always been sort of a symbol to me. If it hadn't been for Joe, Mrs. Arnold would never have bought our good will. I'm so thrilled you agree that it should be kept in trust for another Joe Dakor."

Whiz, who could never be serious for very long, grinned. "Well, now that we're penniless vagrants again, what next?"

"We won't be penniless," Ginny said smugly. "The reason why I was late this morning is that Mrs. Arnold called me as soon as she read the paper. You know how she loves mysteries!"

"We know how she dotes on you," John said, his eyes both teasing and admiring Ginny.

Ginny's own dark eyes twinkled. "She's a wonderful little old lady. And guess what!"

"I can guess," Babs said forlornly. "Carson and Betty are getting married next Saturday and she wanted to have the reception here."

"That's right," Ginny said.

"And that," Whiz said, grinning, "brings us back to vagrancy."

"Oh, no, it doesn't," Ginny told him. "Mrs. Arnold had already read in the paper that the town is taking over the Barn and she thought it was just wonderful. So the reception is going to be at the Inn after all."

"So now," Whiz chuckled, "Mr. Crayne is our best friend. That was a nice piece of business we threw his way."

"Stop interrupting," Babs said crossly. "Ginny has something important to say. I can tell."

"I certainly have," Ginny said. "Mrs. Arnold wants to set us up in the portable lending library business."

"In *what?*" Babs demanded, bewildered. "How can a library be portable?"

Whiz glared at her. "Dope! We have baskets on our bikes, haven't we?"

"We have," John said. "But we'll need some capital." He smiled at Ginny. "Too bad you had to turn that five grand over to Lochinvar."

"We won't need *much* money," Lucy told him and added enthusiastically, "It's the best idea you ever had, Ginny. There are an awful lot of shut-ins and elderly people in Harristown who can't go to the library."

"I know," Ginny said. "And it's the one idea I ever had I think my Great-Aunt Betsy would approve of. She'll become a subscriber, I know. We'll charge them all a dollar apiece for membership cards and rent books to them at the rate of twenty-five cents per week. A lot of them would buy the books they liked instead of returning them."

"Where are we going to get these books?" John asked.

"Why, we'll buy them, of course," Ginny said. "We'll subscribe to all the book clubs and get them more cheaply that way. Some of them we'll have to buy at the publishers' prices when they're first written up in the book reviews. But that doesn't matter. Mrs. Arnold is going to start us with any amount of money we need. She's thrilled to death at the idea of having a finger in the pie."

"I'm thrilled, too," Babs said restlessly. "It'll be a lot more fun biking around town than waiting on tables. We can use sleds in bad weather this winter."

"I'm all for it," Whiz said. "And our parents and teachers will approve of anything we do that exposes us to literature."

"We'll have to have an office," John said thoughtfully, "even if it's just a cubbyhole large enough for a desk, phone and card file."

"Oh, we'll find a place," Ginny said cheerfully. "A basement would do. We'll all be out most of the time keeping the books in circulation, you know."

"No basements," John said firmly. "And no attics. Not with you on the Board of Directors."

"Honestly, John," Ginny cried impatiently. "Why must you always be so cautious? One would think that all I did was go from one mystery to another!"

"That," he said with his slow smile, "is exactly what you seem to do."

WHITMAN BOOKS
FOR BOYS AND GIRLS

NEW STORIES
OF ADVENTURE AND MYSTERY

Up-to-the-minute novels for boys and girls about favorite characters, all popular and well known—

ROY ROGERS and the Outlaws of Sundown Valley
ROY ROGERS and the Ghost of Mystery Rancho
ROY ROGERS and the Gopher Creek Gunman
ROY ROGERS and the Raiders of Sawtooth Ridge

GENE AUTRY and the Badmen of Broken Bow
GENE AUTRY and the Golden Ladder Gang
GENE AUTRY and the Thief River Outlaws
GENE AUTRY and the Redwood Pirates

ZANE GREY'S The Spirit of the Border
ZANE GREY'S The Last Trail

RED RYDER and the Riddle of Roaring Range
RED RYDER and the Adventure at Chimney Rock
RED RYDER and the Secret of the Lucky Mine

BLONDIE and DAGWOOD'S Adventure in Magic
BLONDIE and DAGWOOD'S Marvelous Invention

The books listed above may be purchased at
the same store where you secured this book.

WHITMAN BOOKS
FOR BOYS AND GIRLS

NEW STORIES
OF ADVENTURE AND MYSTERY

THE BOBBSEY TWINS: Merry Days Indoors and Out
THE BOBBSEY TWINS in the Country
THE BOBBSEY TWINS at the Seashore

THE WALTON BOYS in High Country
THE WALTON BOYS in Rapids Ahead
THE WALTON BOYS and Gold in the Snow

TOM STETSON and the Blue Devil
TOM STETSON and the Giant Jungle Ants
TOM STETSON on the Trail of the Lost Tribe

A BOY SAILOR with John Paul Jones
A BOY FIGHTER with Andrew Jackson

GINNY GORDON and the Mystery at the Old Barn
GINNY GORDON and the Mystery of the Missing Heirloom
GINNY GORDON and the Disappearing Candlesticks

TRIXIE BELDEN and the Gatehouse Mystery
TRIXIE BELDEN and the Red Trailer Mystery
TRIXIE BELDEN and the Secret of the Mansion

HARRISTOWN HIGH SCHOOL

Ginny Gordon

John Blaketon